A Break of Day

A Shade of Vampire, Book 7

Bella Forrest

ALSO BY BELLA FORREST:

A Shade of Vampire (Book 1)

A Shade of Blood (Book 2)

A Castle of Sand (Book 3)

A Shadow of Light (Book 4)

A Blaze of Sun (Book 5)

A Gate of Night (Book 6)

Beautiful Monster

For an updated list of Bella's books,
please visit: www.bellaforrest.net

Contents

PROLOGUE: DEREK

We stormed in like a blaze of light, armed not only with swords and guns, but also rage and vengeance. The Elder didn't even see us coming.

When the Ageless had taken me out of The Blood Keep many months ago, I'd promised myself that I would be much stronger when I came back. My vulnerability as a human had only strengthened my resolve to harness and develop whatever power had awakened in me, but I had difficulty focusing without Sofia by my side.

She had always been my calm, my center, and my peace. Without her, all was for naught. The thought that she was still in this godforsaken place, vulnerable because of her pregnancy, pained me beyond measure.

The majority of Elders were still at The Shade when we attacked The Blood Keep. Perhaps they thought that their lair was impervious to any invasion, but this pride had become their downfall.

We showed no mercy as we raided the walls, killing every vampire who didn't belong to our hastily assembled army. If I weren't so desperate to find my wife, I would have marveled at the irony of it all. We had all been enemies. Vampires had always gone after human blood. Hunters had always gone after vampires' heads. And because both of our species combined could not come close to the power and might of the Elders, we had allied ourselves with yet another species; the Hawks, or Guardians as they liked to call themselves.

I still knew little about them, save that they were as ancient and old as the Elders and witches themselves. I didn't trust them one bit, but if they would aid me in rescuing my Sofia, I would take any help that I could get.

I roamed the halls, searching for Sofia. She had been gone from my arms for so long. When I'd found out that we were going to have a child, I'd become even more bent on getting to her. We were going to have a family. Something we wanted for ourselves, maybe after all this havoc.

I didn't know how many I'd felled, or how many had managed to maim me. My entire focus was Sofia. Corinne, powerless as she was, stayed close to me even in the heat of battle. She was the only one who could provide medical assistance to Sofia.

"The Elder has escaped!" Aiden called out as he ran toward me. Although Aiden was one of the most feared hunters the world had ever known, worry for his daughter had worn him down. He was barely able to catch his breath. "It's gone, Derek. It's taken most of the immunes. And I can't find Sofia anywhere!"

My heart stopped beating for a second, but I would not give up until I had Sofia in my arms once again.

I found my hope when one of the hunters ran to me, telling me that Sofia had somehow managed to contact her phone. Even Aiden looked as if he'd regained strength.

"She's somewhere outside," the hunter said. "I'm trying to track her location."

The few minutes it took for her to track Sofia were the longest of my life. It didn't even matter that a bloody battle was happening all around me. Finally, the phone pinged, indicating her location.

My Sofia is alive. It was the only thought that kept me going. The entire world could crumble for all I cared. My wife was alive, and with her, our child.

We rushed to her location and found her lying on the floor of a hut in a puddle of her own water. She was on the verge of giving birth. I ran to her, desperate to feel her within my arms once again.

Corinne immediately took command of the situation and delivered twins. Knowing I had one child with Sofia would have been enough to bring me bliss. Two was a piece of heaven I'd never known I would be given a taste of. In that one moment, I had my family with me—the love of my life and my twins, all within my reach.

But then the devil with the red eyes came to take my son away. And barely a moment later, the Ageless came to whisk my Sofia away too.

To have Sofia taken from my arms sent me spiraling into a pit of despair and sorrow that I could not even begin to describe. I could sense her need for me. Her desperation to be reunited with me mirrored my own, but there was nothing I could do. I could have had all the powers and might in the world, vampire or human, but I was powerless to defend her.

I had failed her. Again.

I wondered then if there was any possible way to escape the

nightmares that continued to plague me. They were starting to unfold right in front of my eyes.

The thought made me shudder.

What happened to a king when he was forced to battle with his queen?

Chapter 1: Sofia

As I stood in the white chambers, a haze descended over me. The flavor of blood was still alive on my tongue, and all I could think about was drinking more. I stooped down to Clara's body and smelt the hot liquid still spilling from her chest. I took a sip but spat it out. Bitter. Disgusting. Nothing like the sweet delicacy she had brought to me.

I stood and was about to search elsewhere when someone seized my arms from behind. I spun around to see a tall man holding me. His eyes were a translucent white and his sagging skin had a yellow tinge.

"Want more blood, Ivana?" His voice was coarse.

"Please!" *Ivana must be my name.*

"Follow me."

He led me into a dark hallway. The décor had changed to black, from the stone floors to the high ceilings—a stark contrast to the room we had just left. I could see perfectly despite the lack of lighting. We walked toward a wide staircase and descended it. The whole place reeked of mold. On the lower floor, we descended another staircase. And another. And another. By the twelfth, I began to smell blood. I was so consumed with anticipation, I stopped noticing my surroundings. The further down we went, the stronger the alluring scent grew.

Eventually we strayed from the levels of staircases and the man opened the door to a dark room. I walked straight in. The scent of fresh blood invaded my nostrils. Then the door slammed shut behind me. I looked around frantically. It didn't take me long to realize that the room was bare.

I ripped at the lock. I scratched against the door. I screamed for release. But my desperation was only met with silence.

How I knew the blood was fresh I didn't fully understand. It was just instinct. I could *feel* its heat seeping through the walls. Its proximity plagued me.

I slumped to the floor and closed my eyes, trying to forget the hunger. But I couldn't; my senses were all too aware. The empty room offered no distractions, so all I could do was sit on the cold stone and pray someone would put me out of my misery.

When the door finally opened, it felt like an eternity had passed. I flew to the door and again found myself face to face with the man with sagging skin.

"You promised me blood!" I screamed, reaching for his neck.

"And I will give you more blood. Orders were that you needed to be ready for it." He remained calm as he knocked my hands away from his throat.

I barely paid attention to his words. He allowed me to step out into the corridor and then withdrew keys from his cloak. He opened the door to the next room.

There lay the source of my torture: a young man with blond hair sleeping in a corner. Without even thinking, I hurled myself toward him and was about to sink my teeth into his neck when his eyes shot open. I gasped as their sharp blue sent a searing pain through my chest.

These eyes. I know these eyes.

The vision of a different blue-eyed stranger, looking down on me with tears and holding me in his arms, flashed through my mind.

Derek.

Waves of memories crashed over me all at once. Complete remembrance settled over me for the first time since arriving at that strange place. *Derek, the birthing, the man with red eyes… where are my babies?* It was all I could do to not fall to the ground and let my emotions take hold of me.

I staggered back, away from the man now huddled in the corner.

"What's wrong, Ivana?"

I'm not Ivana. Sofia. Sofia is my name. Sofia Novak.

"I can't," I breathed out.

"What are you saying, Ivana? You told me you wanted blood."

"My name is Sofia… and I can't drink this man's blood."

I knew at that moment that I had to starve myself of blood. If I let it consume me again, I would lose all my memories. I would forget Derek. I would forget myself. And once I had tasted hot blood gushing directly from a human's throat, I wasn't sure I had it in me to not do it again, and again. I couldn't let the haze envelop me again. I had to fight it.

Now I know what it feels like, Derek. This is what you struggled with. This is why you were so desperate for a cure.

"Oh, you're still not ready for this?" Anger flashed in the man's eyes. "Well, then it's all the more for our little friend here."

Before I could make sense of what was happening, the door swung open and a short vampire rushed into the room. The young man's screams were quickly stifled as the vampire tore through his neck.

I rushed to the corner and gasped when the vampire lifted her head to catch a breath.

Abby.

Her skin was as pale as mine and a darkness had taken over her baby-blue eyes. Hot blood dripping from her lips, she gave me a manic grin before once again drinking from the man's neck.

Seeing Abby, my little sister, this way… I was petrified, but more than that, I was deeply enraged.

They had no right to do this to Abby.

They had no right to do this to me.

Chapter 2: Derek

The sound of the ocean waves did little to help me fall asleep, although Rose had dozed off in my arms hours ago. She breathed gently and her round face had an expression of serenity, as if all was right with the world. As if I was cradling her brother in my arms alongside her… as if her mother…

I choked. I could feel another wave of heat about to come over my body. I placed Rose down on the mattress and walked out onto the terrace outside the beach hut.

Wiping my eyes with the back of my hand, I steadied myself against the banister. I gazed out at the ocean, breathing deeply. The first signs of daybreak were beginning to show on the horizon.

Stay strong, Sofia. Keep your light ablaze. Don't let it die out. I whispered the words, hoping she would somehow hear them through whatever darkness she was now trapped in. It was a mercy that she had passed out before she could witness her son being taken.

Since our separation, although my heart, mind and body were

screaming with despair, I'd had to find the strength within myself to still smile each day for Rose. Her obliviousness was her blessing; it sheltered her from pain. I needed to keep it that way.

My immediate concern had been getting far away from the hunters, Hawks and vampires. Corinne had suggested an old Costa Rican beach hut that she still owned from her student days. I just needed time away from everything to try to patch myself together as much as I could, and gather my thoughts on what I could possibly do next.

Without Corrine, I wasn't sure how I would have handled the situation. Her female instincts and medical knowledge allowed her to help care for Rose in ways that wouldn't have been obvious to me.

My little Rose Red... I looked back to check on my baby. Despite our remote location, I was always in fear for her safety. Corinne had taken my place on the mattress, now cradling Rose in her arms and kissing her forehead. Corinne gave me a weary smile, which I tried to return.

Ibrahim stepped out from the sitting room and walked toward me. Since the Ageless had taken Corrine's powers away, and I was barely in control of my own newfound power, Ibrahim said it was only "right" that he should be here to offer us support. I didn't object because I knew of what value he could be whenever I worked myself up into a fit. Yet I didn't welcome him with open arms either. I knew where his ultimate loyalties lay; with the Ageless, the witch who tore my life apart with a snap of her fingers.

"Beautiful morning, huh?" He spoke quietly as he took a seat on the terrace. "Any further thoughts on leaving?"

I remained silent. We'd had a heated discussion the night before. I'd told him I couldn't leave this place until I'd found someone who was loyal to me and capable of protecting Rose. I wasn't about to risk losing her too. He had volunteered himself, at which point I had laughed in his face and left the room.

"We've just received a text message from Eli," Ibrahim continued. "He's arrived safely at Hawk Headquarters with Shadow and…"

Before he could finish his sentence, I whirled round and stared at the phone in horror. "I thought I told you to keep that damned thing switched off! It's meant for emergencies, not for communicating with the hunters. Do you realize how easy it will be for them to track us now?"

I snatched the phone from his hand, jumped off the terrace, and ran toward the ocean, hurling it into the waves. Then I ripped off my clothes and dove in myself, desperate for relief.

I knew I was overreacting. Eli knew what this privacy meant to me and would have texted only from a secure location. But I couldn't help myself. I was burning up inside and no amount of water could extinguish me.

I lay on my back and allowed the waves to carry me. A morning breeze blew over me. I looked up at the clear sky, feeling weightless. Only a few months ago, I would have given anything to be lying here, not afraid of the sun that was about to rise. And then we had found the cure.

Is this to be my life? To rise up only to be brought back down to my knees, shattered into shards?

We'd only been at the hut for a few nights, but it was time for me to leave. Ready or not, I couldn't remain stagnant on this beach any longer. There wasn't a second of the day when my mind wasn't plagued with thoughts of Sofia and our son. Ben. That was the name Sofia had wanted for our first boy. I needed to reach Aiden and work out a plan.

I felt sand beneath my back; the waves had carried me back to shore. I sat up and someone called my name. Corrine approached and sat down next to me.

"Derek, I know how hard this is for you. But you know better than I that you can't keep delaying this decision. The longer Sofia is in the clutches of the Elders… Look, either take Rose with you to Hawk Headquarters—"

"You know that's impossible. Her grandfather may be there, but that place is still under the control of Arron, whom we obviously can't trust."

"Then leave her here with me and Ibrahim."

I snorted, then motioned to stand up and walk back to the hut, aware that Rose was now alone with Ibrahim. But Corrine held on to my arm and yanked me back down.

"If Ibrahim wanted to harm or kidnap Rose, he could do it even in your presence. There's nothing stopping him from grabbing her right from your arms and vanishing back to The Sanctuary. I know Ibrahim. And I trust him. He's here to help us. And you need to get to Aiden as soon as possible."

"How can you expect me to trust him when his mistress just…" I trailed off, memories of that night threatening to choke me up again.

"The Ageless came for Sofia. Not your children. I'm telling you, you won't find anyone more capable than Ibrahim of protecting your daughter and me. If Ibrahim says that Rose will be safe, then she will be. She will have the protection of the witches' realm, because Ibrahim is acting as The Sanctuary's emissary. Whoever crosses him will answer to the Ageless herself."

I looked into Corrine's brown eyes and reluctantly saw truth in them. Ibrahim could outmatch any vampire, Hawk or hunter. I remained silent for a few minutes, diverting my attention back to the ocean. The sun had now risen above the horizon, warming my skin.

I was about to speak again when Ibrahim appeared next to us. He was carrying Rose, who had now woken up. He handed her to me and said, "You can go to the hunters, Derek. I swear that Rose won't be harmed."

I looked down into my baby's beautiful green eyes and ached inside. She looked up at me with wide-eyed innocence. I kissed her warm cheeks and stroked her fine black hair, then pulled her close against my chest. *If anything should happen to you while I'm gone, I will have nothing left to live for.*

Chapter 3: Sofia

Once Abby had almost finished sucking the young man dry, the male vampire grabbed my arm and pulled me out of the room, leaving Abby alone to finish her feast.

"One thing you would do well to learn sooner rather than later is that we Elders are not the most patient of creatures," he said, tightening his grip on my arm.

My heart began racing. *So this is an Elder.* He led me along the hallway, turned right into another chamber and slammed the door behind us. It was much larger than the last room and bare inside save for a table on which rested an assortment of whips. I struggled against his grasp but he held me tight.

He forced me to the ground, ripped the back of my dress open and poured a cold liquid onto my skin, which began stinging. Then came the lashes. One after another, beating against my spine and tearing into my flesh.

"Stop... Stop... Please!" I could barely utter the words through the pain.

He stopped only after my back had become numb from the torture. Then he grabbed me and pulled me to a standing position next to him.

"Now, you need to heal. But first I must change vessel. All this unnecessary exertion has rendered this old one useless."

He dragged me out of the room, back toward the black marble staircases. Despite my stumbling and tripping against him, we climbed down several more levels.

We entered yet another chamber, this time with a young blonde vampire wearing a tattered red dress. The Elder sat me down on the ground, removed his black cloak, and gave it to me to hold. Then, without warning, his decrepit form collapsed in a heap. The female vampire let out a bloodcurdling scream, then her neck clicked, her face contorted and she stood up as if nothing had happened. She walked over to me and grabbed the black cloak, throwing it over her shoulders. Then she pulled me to my feet just as harshly as the man now dead on the floor had set me down.

"That old vessel was second-hand already. This one is much more comfortable. Now, let's fix you."

The lashes and the shock of what I'd just witnessed made me dizzy. I tried to steady my legs but fell to the floor and everything faded to black.

****

When I came to, I found myself lying on a cot in a room not dissimilar from the one we had left Abby in. My back was still causing me so much agony that it sent my head reeling again.

Sitting in the corner was an old woman—a human, I knew instantly. Her blood smelled irresistible. *Sweet. Succulent.* The Elder sat at the opposite end of the room, watching me.

"This is an immune. We haven't turned her yet, as you can see. I'm sure you've noticed how much sweeter and richer her blood smells? You want to stop the pain? You drink."

The old woman whimpered and cowered in the corner.

"I can't," I said through gritted teeth. It took every ounce of restraint to not fly at the woman's throat.

The Elder stood up and dragged me closer to the woman, pushing my head down so her scent was now intoxicating me. I shook my head violently.

"No... No... Get off of me!" I stamped down hard on the Elder's foot, making her lose balance. This gave me the five seconds I needed to flee through the open door.

I had no idea where I was going and the pain slowed me down. I headed back toward the staircases and then upward, hoping to lose myself in the maze of dark hallways and chambers. But it didn't take long until I bumped into a second vampire—another Elder inhabiting another old vessel. I could tell this time due to the yellowish tinge of the body.

He caught my arm and pulled me down, holding me against the stairs until the Elder chasing me had caught up.

"Thank you," she said, addressing him. "I'll take charge from here." Then she turned to me. Her eyes rolled in their sockets and her mouth split into a lopsided grin. "Very well. You won't cooperate? We'll just have to make you our very own little puppet then."

She pulled out a vial of red liquid from her cloak, and before I could even react, she yanked open my mouth and poured it in. Its sweetness tantalized my tongue and the effect was instant; my wounds stopped aching. And, for the second time in the past few hours, I lost all consciousness.

****

This time when I opened my eyes, my surroundings felt strangely familiar. I lay on a cold stone slab. I sat bolt upright and glanced around. I was in the largest and innermost chamber of The Shade's Sanctuary.

The exact spot where Derek woke up. Where I first met him. Where it all started.

The torches fixed to the high walls gave off a dim glow. A wave of relief washed over me. I was home. For all I knew, Derek could be within less than a mile. But then the reality hit me full force. *How did that Elder bring me here? Why on earth would it bring me home?* I knew that the answers to these questions would bring me neither joy nor relief.

The chamber seemed empty, although there was a strange round hole about fifteen feet away from me. I stood up cautiously. Just as I motioned to walk over to it, a deep voice I knew so well echoed around the room.

"Sofia."

Xavier! A figure stirred in the shadows in a far corner of the room. I was ecstatic to see a dear friend. I rushed toward him to pull him into an embrace. But as I got closer, joy turned to horror.

Translucent eyes. A manic grin.

"Xavier!" I screamed.

Xavier fell to the ground, twitching. A freezing cold enveloped me, seeping into my bones. I managed to scream for a few seconds, but then I lost my voice. I couldn't move my tongue. I couldn't open my mouth. I couldn't move any part of my body. I felt trapped in my own body as a dark presence closed in around me.

Then I heard my own voice speak.

"No, darling. I'm not Xavier. Just the darkness that consumed him. The same one that has now consumed you."

Chapter 4: Derek

Early the next morning, I packed up a few key belongings. I made sure to leave behind a spare phone, instructing Corrine and Ibrahim to contact me only in an emergency. Then, after holding Rose one last time, I headed further inland, to the city of Liberia. There I used a telephone box to make contact with Aiden and, six hours later, I found myself boarding a helicopter bound for Hawk Headquarters.

During the flight, I tried to stop thinking about what Sofia and my son could be going through. I tried to stop thinking about what was beyond my control. If I was to think clearly and not be a constant fire hazard at Headquarters, I had to keep my emotions in check.

On my arrival, Aiden was waiting for me on the landing pad. The lines in his face had grown deeper over the past few days and he had dark circles under his eyes. In spite of this, he smiled and gave me a brief hug. Then his brows creased with worry. "My granddaughter?"

"Rose is safe with Corrine and Ibrahim, at least for the moment. I wouldn't have left her if I'd thought that she wasn't safe."

"Rose," he said softly. "I wish I could have seen her."

"You know why I left her behind. Right now, we're working with Arron and the Hawks blindly because we have no choice. But there are still far too many things about their motives that we don't understand. This is no place to bring a newborn."

Pain flickered in his eyes, but he composed himself. He was a man well practiced at switching off his emotions. We marched toward the main building.

We reached his office and shut ourselves inside. Sitting at the table waiting for us was Arron. When he saw me enter, his lips curled.

"Welcome back, Derek."

I nodded curtly but said nothing. I would have preferred to talk privately with Aiden, but Arron knew more about Cruor, the vampire realm, than Aiden, and he certainly had more influence. I remembered how, though he had not accompanied us personally when we stormed The Blood Keep, he had armed us with dozens of Hawks from Aviary.

I took a seat opposite Aiden, who looked grimly at me before launching the discussion. "Firstly, Sofia. Based on what the Ageless told you, we can only assume she's in Cruor."

"There are three gates that allow passage into that realm," Arron continued. "One at The Underground; one at The Shade; and one at The Blood Keep. Now, at the time the witch took Sofia, we were storming the Keep, so I doubt very much she would have transported Sofia to that particular gate. So the witch either sent Sofia to The Shade or The Underground, after which an Elder would have taken her through the portal and into Cruor."

"Why do they want her?" I asked, terrified to hear Arron's answer.

"Isn't that obvious? She's an immune. An immune's blood is rare sustenance to their kind. You remember the effect it had on you? What it felt like drinking it?"

I shuddered. I remembered drinking Sofia's blood all too clearly.

"Let's cut to the chase," Aiden said. "To rescue my daughter, it seems the only way is to force entry into Cruor and retrieve her. One of the many problems with this is that not even Arron knows if it's possible for a 'non-Elder' to enter without assistance."

"And Ben? My son?"

Aiden heaved a sigh and ran a hand through his hair. "It's still a mystery to us. We've made no progress in tracking Kiev. Truth be told, I have no clue where to even start. We have virtually no background on Kiev other than his stay at The Blood Keep. And we searched the whole place since he kidnapped Ben. The Keep is now empty, save for a few dogs. Kiev too could be in Cruor for all we know."

I looked at Arron. "And you have nothing to add?"

"No."

I breathed deeply. *Ignore your emotions. They won't help find your family. Focus, Novak. Focus.*

"All right. For now, it appears that our only option is to put all our focus on Cruor. We'll need the assistance of the Hawks again. God knows what we'll find ourselves faced with at the end of that portal, if we even manage to enter it."

I was interrupted by a sharp knock at the door. Aiden got up to open it. When Vivienne stepped into the room, my heart leapt. I jumped up and pulled her into my arms.

"Derek, I've been so worried about you," she said breathlessly. "When you didn't return Eli's text... I didn't know what to think."

"I'm just about hanging on, Vivienne. I'm glad you arrived

safely." I kissed the top of her head. "What about the others who were headed here?"

"Claudia, Cameron, Zinnia, Gavin, Eli, Shadow, and Xavier's brother Landis, they're all here."

"What of Ashley, Liana, Yuri and Xavier?"

Her lower lip trembled and tears filled her eyes. She looked down at the floor. That was enough of an answer. I wanted to comfort her, but we had no time for it now. We had to stop mourning the situation and put all our efforts into facing it.

I sat back down, anxious to resume our discussion. Storming The Keep was one thing. Barging into a different realm was entirely another. I knew the only person with true power to help us was the Ageless. It was our misfortune that she was the one person who was certain to never help us.

Just then, there was another knock at the door.

"Come in!" Aiden snapped. A young hunter rushed in. "What do you want?"

He lifted up a phone. "For Mr. Novak. Someone called Corrine is on the line."

My heart leapt into my throat as I snatched the phone from him. "Corrine?"

"Derek. I feel mad saying this out loud, but… Sofia just showed up at the hut."

Chapter 5: Sofia

Now that the Elder had taken over my body, I was in a constant state of cold. The chill had settled within the marrow of my bones and made them ache. My eyes stung, yet I couldn't blink. My vision was blurred; I could still see, but not clearly. I wanted to gasp for breath, yet I was not in control of my own windpipe.

Leave me… please! I begged.

My mouth opened in response.

"We have much work to do together, you and I."

I shivered internally.

"And besides, you're far too sumptuous a vessel to let go of before your expiry." This time my body trembled—it was the Elder trembling through me, as if experiencing pleasure.

My legs carried me out of the temple and into the garden outside. The moon's rays shone down on the clearing, allowing me to make out the shadows of three figures sitting in a circle on the lawn. As we drew close, I was horrified to see that I recognized all of them:

Ashley, Liana and Yuri. Only they were not the same vampires I knew, just as I was no longer the Sofia they knew.

My legs folded beneath me and I dropped to the ground next to Ashley.

"Continue where we were. Before I left to change."

I wondered if my friends had thoughts like I had. Whether they too were horrified to see me. If they were, I could not tell. Their eyes remained unfocussed and their faces void of expression. I assumed they saw the same in me.

It was Liana who spoke next, anger in her voice. "Did I not warn you that this might happen if too many of us rushed through at once? We are expiring too many vessels. We are exerting them far too much. And we are forgetting the purpose of our visit; we came here for a harvest."

"I agree with you. If we were back on the other side of the gate, we'd never dream of engaging in such activities." Ashley addressed me. "We are becoming complacent, forgetting that vessels are a far more precious commodity now than they were only a short while ago, thanks to the queen here." She waved a hand toward me in disgust.

"I will ensure that this *queen* realizes her mistake, have no doubts about that," my voice replied.

"We must call a ban on spoiling any more vessels," Ashley said.

Yuri, who had been swigging from a bottle of wine, looked agitated. "We have been starving ourselves for too long! We're already abstaining from immunes. To hell with more austerity! There are still plenty of vessels remaining on this island. And when we run out of supply? We go forth and create more."

"Mindless fool. You know it's not as easy as that any more. And what about all the human blood we have needlessly wasted?" Liana

24

said. "I can't stand watching it spilled on the ground by filthy game hounds! It's fresh, hot blood that we should bring back for our own sustenance. We've had enough amusement. Now we must see to the preservation of our kind."

From the way we were all speaking, it was now obvious to me that these were the key leaders of the whole operation. But the decisive tone my voice took on next made me realize that the Elder possessing me was even a step higher than the other three.

"We will call a ban on any further wastage; both humans and vessels." Yuri opened his mouth to protest, but my voice bulldozed over him. "To accomplish this, all Elders—save for the four of us and a few dozen others who you think are best suited to assist us—must return through the gate. We can call on reinforcements as and when they become necessary."

Ashley and Liana nodded in approval.

"Then, we organize the creation of more vessels. Only once we have collected enough to fill Cruor's chambers will we resume our festivities. Is this understood?"

Yuri's face twitched but it was clear that he was not about to argue.

My voice continued. "For now, we'll keep all humans and vessels already on this island as they are currently situated: the humans in the lower levels of The Cells; the vessels in the upper levels. Once we've completed our procreation, we'll call on more Elders to come back through the gate and help us transport them all back to Cruor in one swoop."

"And the Hawks…" Liana began.

"The plan for the Guardians remains as it was," I said, looking at Liana. "Go now and wait for me by the Port."

We all stood up at once. Ashley and Yuri began walking toward

The Vale; Liana to the Port; and myself toward The Cells. Using my vampire speed, the Elder rushed us past the giant redwoods until we arrived at the large wooden entrance.

As my Elder had mentioned, they had evacuated the humans from The Catacombs and stuffed them all into The Cells for ease of access. It sickened me to see the number of humans they held in each cell; they were caged like animals. Those who weren't sleeping or unconscious looked up at me as I passed them.

"Sofia! Oh, thank God!"

"Please, help us!"

"Mom, look! Queen Sofia is back! I told you she'd come for us!"

I couldn't even turn my head to see who was calling out to me. I was sure I heard the voice of a little girl among them. The Elder continued to march my body forward. The lighting was so dim that I doubted they could even see my face to understand that I had been possessed. They would think that I was ignoring their plight.

These were my people; they were dependent on Derek and me to rule them and give them protection. A wave of guilt hit me, crushing me into dust. Then fury boiled within me unlike any I had ever felt before.

This time when the Elder addressed me, he didn't use my voice to speak out loud. It was as if he had read my thoughts and felt my emotions. I heard his hissing voice within my head.

"Save your sentiments for later, girl. I promise you'll find better use for them."

You won't get away with this, you snake, I screamed in my head. Tears would have fallen from my eyes had I been in control of them. I thanked the heavens that, at least for the time being, no more blood was to be spilled.

After a few more minutes of this torture, we stopped in front of a cell. Inside, a person slumped on the floor. She crawled to the bars and started whimpering.

"Please, feed me! My stomach is burning! I'll do whatever you want!"

She was a young woman wearing a torn black gown. Her face was brown with dirt and she looked like she hadn't eaten in days.

"Silence, witch!" my cold voice said.

If she was a witch, I wondered to myself why on earth she allowed them to treat her this way. The Elder answered my curiosity within my own head.

Not all witches are as powerful as your Corrine.

It was disturbing to know that my every thought was exposed to this kind of evil.

I continued to speak: "I will feed you. But in return, you must polish my vessel. The same treatment as the last vessel we sent to you."

The witch lost no time in gathering herself up from the ground. She staggered to the corner of her cell and started mixing some kind of concoction together—what exactly, I couldn't see. Then she murmured a chant for several minutes, walked back over to the bars and threw a handful of powder into my eyes. The powder felt like acid and in my head, I cried out in pain. But after a few seconds the stinging subsided and my vision was as clear as it had been before my possession.

She held up a mirror. My eyes were exactly as I remembered them. My face also looked the same as when I first discovered I'd been turned, back in the white chambers. No crooked expression. I certainly didn't look like an Elder was inhabiting me.

I reached for a black box that was lying on the ground in the empty cell next to the witch's. I withdrew a piece of dry bread and threw it toward her. She snatched it and began eating ravenously.

Then, without another word, I turned around and headed toward the exit. The second time we passed by the humans, they were far more subdued. Most didn't bother calling my name. Instead I heard low mutterings. It cut me to the core to realize that they must have already accepted that I had abandoned them.

Once we'd exited The Cells, the Elder started speaking to me again.

"Now, help me understand where your lover could have gone."

Memories flashed before my eyes; all of them involving locations. After a few seconds, it dawned on me. *He's accessing my memories.* The flashing stopped, leaving a vision of a small beach hut. *But I've never been to this place. This isn't even my memory.*

"Aha," the Elder hissed. "He wouldn't be fool enough to go running to the Hawks' protection. He was with the witch on the night of the birth. This would have been the natural option."

Then I remembered that the memories contained within my head were not all my own. *Vivienne's memory.*

"Once we have arrived there, I will give you back control of your body. You are to follow my every command. And never forget, I'm right here with you."

Chapter 6: Sofia

Not my husband… and my babies…

Panic set my mind on fire. I couldn't think straight. Fear, despair and rage consumed me all at once. I wanted to scream at the top of my lungs.

Instead, I rushed toward the port. Waiting for us there, peeking out of the hatch of a small submarine, was Liana. I climbed in and we both took a seat near the controls. I grabbed a map from the dashboard and hovered my finger over it for a few moments until I pointed to a coastal area in southern Costa Rica. I picked up a pen and drew a mark against it, then handed it to Liana.

"This is the location. If we wish to reach there before the next century, you must loosen control of your vessel so that she can navigate the ship. But keep close watch on her. She is loyal to the Novaks and we have no time for detours."

You bastard. You snake.

I stood up and made my way to the back of the submarine. We

had barely sat down on one of the benches when we lurched forward. The Elder's mind must have been preoccupied with other matters since it chose not to respond to my insults.

My thoughts turned to Liana. *The submarine is moving. My dear friend is back in control of herself again.* I feared she'd risk her life by attempting to veer us off course, hoping that her Elder wouldn't notice. She'd be a fool to even try; she'd be caught the moment she entertained the thought.

I wished that I could walk back into the control room and embrace her. It felt like an eternity since I'd come in contact with even a shred of humanity. I longed for a warm embrace, the squeeze of a hand, reassuring me that we would make it through this ordeal. I'd been frozen with fear and doubt for so long, I was desperate for anything that could help keep my fire alive. Darkness threatened to close in on me at any moment. Every second was a battle to prevent the haze from settling over me again.

The fact that I had no clue as to what the Elder planned to do with my family once we arrived caused my mind to spiral into a black abyss of terrifying possibilities. *Do they want to turn my children too, or keep them for their blood? Will they bring them back to Cruor and make them grow up in the darkness of the storage chambers? What will they do to Derek? Will they harm him just to spite me, or will they find use for him as a vessel?*

Several hours must have passed while I remained seated in the same spot, quivering slightly. The reason for my parasite's silence dawned on me. *The Elder is taking pleasure in my fear. My despair is its strength. I can't give it that.*

The thought of depriving the Elder of pleasure summoned a strength that I'd thought I had lost. I forced myself to imagine living happily with my family, sheltered from harm. *Derek bought that beautiful beachfront villa. When I find my way back to him, he'll be waiting on the porch. He'll be holding our children, one in each arm. I'll run up and shower them with kisses...* I smiled internally. A warm feeling of peace spread through me.

My body stopped quivering and the Elder made me stand up and start pacing around the small compartment, as though trying to distract itself from my thoughts.

I remained pacing for another hour until the submarine thudded to a halt. Liana appeared through the door and said, "We're about half a mile from the location you marked. It's best we keep our distance and you travel by foot from here."

I nodded. Then I reached up for the hatch, pushed it open, and slid myself out, dropping into shallow waters. It ached to leave Liana behind with no assurance that I would ever see her again. And what would become of Ashley, Yuri, Xavier and all the other vampires and humans of The Shade? I felt myself in danger of sinking again.

Stay strong, Sofia. You're no stranger to storms. The waves may rage, but you can rise above them.

As we approached within ten feet of the hut, the Elder finally spoke to me.

"Remember my warning. There will be moments when I will release you from my grasp, but when I issue a command, whatever it is, you obey."

Then he made me start banging on the door frantically.

"Please, open the door!" I heard my voice shout.

After a few moments, footsteps hurried closer and a familiar face appeared. Corrine. On seeing me, she let out a small scream and her eyes widened with shock.

"Sofia! What? How?"

"I'll explain! Please just let me inside!" Cold tears streamed down my face, forced out of me by the Elder.

Corrine swung the door open. She led me to a small sitting room and pushed me down into a chair. I was breathing quickly.

"I managed to escape Cruor!"

"How?"

"A vampire. I don't know who he is. All I know is that he was a rogue, a traitor to their kind. He took pity on me when I told him I had young children. He helped me back through the portal."

"You're a..."

"They turned me. I don't know how. When I came to consciousness, I'd been turned already. I was craving blood."

As Corrine stared into my eyes, I wished that she could see them for what they were: hollow sockets, gates to a prison, behind which my soul was crying out for her to understand.

"How did you get here?"

I stood up abruptly. "Where's Derek?"

"He-he left for Hawk Headquarters just recently."

A dark-haired man with a goatee stepped into the sitting room and eyed me. The Elder made me ignore him.

"My babies. I want to see my babies!" I said.

When Corrine cast her eyes to the ground, my heart sank to my stomach.

"Sofia, your baby daughter—Rose, Derek named her—is sleeping in the bedroom next door." Corrine paused, tears welling in her eyes. "Your son, Ben. We... I-I lost him." She sank to the floor, weeping. "I don't know how you'll ever forgive me."

I gasped—this time audibly. The Elder had now released his control of my body to allow me to show a mother's grief. I fell to the ground alongside Corrine and begged her to explain.

"The vampire with red eyes. He came so fast, I couldn't fight him off," she choked. "He snatched Ben right from my arms. We still don't know where he took him."

Corrine wrapped her arms around me. This time, my own tears were allowed to flood. I sobbed and trembled against her. I was now desperate to see my daughter. But I knew I needed to stay as far away from Rose as possible, so when Corrine led me to Rose's bedroom, I stepped back.

Move forward! The Elder's hissing voice echoed in my head.

I refused. I stepped back toward the exit of the hut, forcing the Elder to jolt me forward toward Rose's bedroom.

Corrine paused, eyeing me closely. I prayed to the heavens that she had become suspicious.

"Please! I need to see my daughter!" my voice said.

We entered the dark bedroom and stood around my baby's cot. *So this is you, Rose. My beautiful baby girl. So peaceful.*

Isn't she beautiful, Sofia? the Elder asked. *She will soon regret the day her mother crossed the Elders.*

To my horror, my arms shot down into the crib, picked Rose up, and began cradling her.

CHAPTER 7: DEREK

I couldn't believe my ears.

"*What?*"

"Sofia. She's here. She arrived about an hour ago," Corrine repeated.

"How?"

"Just get back here. You can ask her yourself."

When Corrine hung up, I pinched my arm to check that I hadn't fallen into some kind of cruel daydream. Then I looked wildly around the room until my eyes found Aiden's. His face mirrored what I was feeling. He grabbed the phone from me and within a few seconds was shouting for a helicopter. Then he turned to me and croaked, "Bring her back here, Derek. I need to see her."

I dashed outside to the launch pad and hurled myself into the aircraft, whose engine was already humming. Discarding all caution, I gave the coordinates of the beach hut to the pilot and we took off.

A hundred questions crowded my mind, but most of all, the most intense sense of relief I'd ever felt in my life flooded through me. *My Sofia, my light. You're alive.* I wondered if they'd already told her about Ben. I felt sick imagining how she would have reacted. But somehow, now that she was back, the task of finding Ben seemed more surmountable than just a few minutes ago.

I could barely sit still throughout the flight, fidgeting and asking the pilot how much longer until our arrival. I felt paranoid that somehow she'd be snatched away again during the time it took me to travel to her. Ibrahim was the Ageless' ally. What if he decided to alert the witch and she came to reclaim Sofia? I closed my eyes and tried to breathe deeply. My whole being ached to hold Sofia in my arms, run my fingers through her long hair and feel her soft lips against mine.

When the helicopter started its descent, I could barely contain myself. As soon as it touched down on the beach, I jumped out and raced to the hut. Corrine opened the door. She looked exhausted and her face was filled with concern. I barely greeted her as I pushed past her and entered the sitting room.

"Sofia!"

My vision blurred when Sofia whispered my name and rushed toward me, placing her arms around my neck. I had to fight to hold back the tears as I held her waist and pulled her shaking body against mine. I wondered why she was so cold. I ran my hands up and down the length of her back, hoping my rubbing would warm her. I placed my lips on her collarbone, then her neck, her cheek, and finally her mouth. Her tears wet my face as I kissed her hungrily, my tongue pushing between her lips. I had been starved of her for too long. My body was now coursing with levels of passion I could barely contain.

I knew that she would still be very sensitive from the birthing. I had to be careful with her. But it was clear she felt the same passion when she put her hands beneath my shirt and ran them up my torso. I was about to pick her up and carry her into the spare bedroom for some privacy when I felt it: a sharp stab in my lower lip. I let go of her and took a step back, confused. I touched my lip and saw blood on my finger. Then I looked more closely at Sofia's pale face.

"Sofia?"

Her eyes still filled with tears, she opened her mouth and bared fangs.

"I'm so sorry," she sobbed.

"You're... how?" I gripped her shoulders and looked at her desperately, praying that my eyes were deceiving me.

"I-I just woke up and saw the fangs. I craved blood. I don't understand how. I thought I was an immune!"

My head started reeling. Doubts assailed me about what her transformation would mean for her, our family, our future. *Will the cure work on a vampire created directly by the Elders? Is that even a risk I would allow her to take?*

"How on earth did you escape?"

"A rogue vampire, one of the vessels—he helped me. He was a servant to the Elders and had their trust. Whenever he came to my cell to feed me, I begged him to have mercy on me. Eventually I guess I got through to him and he smuggled me back through the gate into The Shade."

"The Shade? But that place is swarming with Elders! How could they not have noticed you?"

She looked up at me wearily. "Please, Derek, no more questions about what I've been through. I don't want to think about it any more. I'm here now. Isn't that enough?" She placed one cool hand on my face and tugged at my shirt. Then she whispered in my ear. "I can't stand it any more. Can't you see I'm dying for you? Our time

36

together was much too short."

Although my mind was still burning with questions and anxiety, I gave in to her request. I determined to shut everything out and just focus on Sofia, my beautiful wife who had returned to me. I tried to pretend that at that moment in time, nothing else existed except our two beating hearts.

I picked her up and walked to the bedroom. Placing her feet gently down on the ground, I undressed her, kissing any part of her body my lips could brush against. When I hesitated, she said, "You won't hurt me, Derek. Remember I'm a vampire now."

Then she pulled off my clothes, lay on the bed, and, gripping my hair, pulled me down toward her.

Although Sofia had lost her warmth, she was still as beautiful as I had remembered her. No matter how long I lay there with her, her body intertwined with mine, it felt like my appetite for her would never be satiated. And it appeared that she felt the same way.

Until a strange darkness flickered in her eyes, and she began to draw blood.

I thought back to when I was a vampire, how much control it had taken to not force blood from her whenever we slept together. But, although it had been a herculean task, I had managed it. Surely it should be easier for Sofia to not give into the darkness. After all, she was the one who had trained *me* to control my cravings.

Why are you doing this, Sofia?

Chapter 8: Sofia

As soon as I woke the next morning, I found myself getting out of bed and walking to the window to pull down the blinds, blocking the rising sun from streaming into the room. Then I turned to look at Derek, who was still asleep in bed. His body was covered with bruises and bite marks. Horror and guilt surged through me.

The Elder had released me from his control a number of times since Derek had entered the hut, allowing me to display my own emotions. But once my teeth had started sinking into Derek's flesh, his blood seeping into my mouth, I knew the Elder had taken back full control. I'd seen the pain in Derek's face. His eyes had betrayed that I was hurting him on a much deeper level than merely physically.

I had tried to cry out on several occasions. Each time, my voice had been choked back. All I could do was pray that the evil inhabiting me would find some speck of mercy and make me leave the hut, disappear to some place a thousand miles away. I might as well have prayed for my best friend Ben to come back to life.

Derek stirred on the bed and groaned. He opened his eyes and when he saw me standing by the window he managed to smile as though nothing had happened.

"Good morning, beautiful." He beckoned me over to the bed. I lay down next to him and he pulled me in for a cuddle. Kissing the top of my head, he asked, "Did you see Rose? Her eyes, they're just like yours."

"Of course I saw her. She looks so healthy. You and Corrine have been taking good care of her."

"Corrine has some friends in the village down the road. One of them has a baby of her own and she offered to breastfeed Rose. Corrine and Ibrahim have been taking her daily—Ibrahim is... well, that's a long story."

It pained me to think that I'd never even experienced the simple pleasure of feeding my own children. And I never would so long as I remained a vampire.

Derek began explaining to me everything that had transpired since I was first taken to The Blood Keep: how he'd escaped The Keep himself, his stay at The Sanctuary with Ibrahim and the Ageless, the Guardians... His story blew my mind. He was talking fast and I wanted to stop him and ask questions, but frustratingly, my mouth remained sealed. He'd been talking for over an hour until his story reached the part where I was taken by the witch, at which point he paused. He tilted my head up with his hand and his bright blue eyes bored into mine.

"I thought I'd lost you, Sofia. I can't tell you how scared I was." His arms tightened around me and he placed a tender kiss on my forehead.

You did lose me, Derek. I'm not your Sofia.

After a moment of silence, he cleared his throat and continued. "Aiden asked me to bring you to Headquarters. He desperately wants to see you. But at the time he made this request, he was too overcome with emotion to realize what a terrible idea that is... especially now you're..." Derek's voice trailed off. "We don't yet understand what the Guardians' true motives are. I don't know how Arron would react to seeing you as a vampire and I'm not about to take any risks with you. Even staying in this hut is dangerous now the hunters know its location. We need to find a new place to stay on a different coast as soon as possible."

"Derek." I heard my voice interrupt him softly. "I really, really want to go to Headquarters. I want to see my dad."

Derek brushed the back of my head with his hand.

"Sofia, of course I understand that. But there's no reason to risk going to Headquarters just to see your father. Aiden's busy trying to locate Ben, but I'm sure he can fly here for a few hours to see you."

"No, Derek." I pulled away from his arms, sitting upright on the bed. "I want to go to Headquarters. It's not just Aiden I want to see." Memories of people I'd seen at Headquarters during my stay there whirred through my brain. "There's also Zinnia, Craig, Julian..."

Utter confusion spread across Derek's face. "Craig? Zinnia? Sofia, is this supposed to be a joke? Because it's not funny. I'm not getting it."

"I just want to go to Headquarters. I feel safer there than in some little hut."

"But listen..."

"And if you won't take me, I'll leave you and go there myself."

CHAPTER 9: DEREK

Sofia just blackmailed me.

I was in a state of shock as I walked out of the bedroom and stood in the sitting room, grabbing the back of a chair to steady my hands. I'd left Sofia sitting on the bed after promising her that I'd consider her request. I'd told her that I needed to discuss some things with Corrine and Ibrahim.

Since I had known Sofia, she had never threatened me in this way. And over what? Her insistence on visiting Headquarters was completely irrational. Sofia had never been whimsical. When faced with any decision, she always weighed the pros and cons.

Has she lost her mind? Maybe the shock of turning has made her mentally unstable. Maybe she just needs time to recover. There was only one thing I knew for sure: the person sitting in my bedroom was not the girl I'd married.

A vision from one of my nightmares flashed before my eyes, nightmares that still plagued me on the rare occasions that I slept.

Sofia stood in a fountain outside the witch's temple in The Shade. Her long hair covered her face like a curtain. Her body swayed from side to side, as if moved by the breeze.

I called out her name. No response.

"What's wrong with you?"

I started walking toward her. As I got closer, the fountain's clear water turned to red. A shriek emanated from Sofia's mouth as she flipped her hair aside to reveal her face.

Her eyes were black as a coal pit. Blood dripped from her lips. Her skin was cracked and aged.

"What have you done with my Sofia?"

I found myself breathing heavily just remembering the dream. *Are these simply my worst fears playing tricks on my mind? Or could these nightmares actually bear some meaning?* I shuddered the thought away and wrapped a robe around my body.

Maybe vampires created in Cruor just find it far more difficult to control themselves, and that's why even Sofia is struggling. She helped me out of my darkness. Now it's my turn to help her.

I pushed open the door to the bedroom we had transformed into a nursery for Rose. Corrine was sitting on a sofa, holding little Rose on her lap. Ibrahim had his arm around Corrine's waist, but quickly removed it.

Corrine looked up at me.

"Thank God you've come here without her. I would have said something last night, but I didn't have the heart to interrupt when I saw you two standing there."

"Why?" Her anxiety took me by surprise.

"Come closer." She grabbed my hand and pulled my head down so that my ear was less than an inch away from her lips. Then she continued in a voice that was barely louder than a breath. "Ibrahim and I… We've been discussing. We don't think Rose should be in the same house as Sofia. Hell, not even in the same country. I have some more contacts, old classmates, down in Argentina. Ibrahim will come with us of course…"

"What is it that you've noticed about Sofia?" I interrupted.

"Shh! Speak more softly. Don't tell me that you haven't noticed, Derek. You're not that thick, I pray. There's something very wrong with your wife." The witch looked at me with fear in her eyes. "I don't know what, I can't put my finger on it. But there's a feeling in my bones that I can't shake. She's not mentally stable."

"The way she looked at Rose," Ibrahim whispered. "At first her eyes were filled with motherly affection, but the next moment, a darkness had settled over them… only to vanish again. She's not in control of her own nature. She's unpredictable."

This conversation was doing nothing to allay my fears.

"All right. I agree," I breathed. "Take Rose. Take her far away. I'm trusting you and Ibrahim to guard her with your lives. Remember to bring the phone with you."

Corrine looked relieved. "What about you? What will you do, Derek?"

"I need to stay here with Sofia. I need to find a cure for her. And I need to find my son." I looked at the warlock. "Ibrahim, how do I know that the Ageless won't come for Sofia again?"

"You don't," he said simply. "But the fact that your wife has been here for more than fifteen hours and the Ageless hasn't showed up suggests to me that, for whatever reason, she's not interested in handing Sofia back to Cruor."

Like a cup of water in the desert, his words gave me a dose of relief.

Then Corrine stood up, wrapped a blanket around Rose, and handed her to me. I kissed my baby girl goodbye for the second time in less than seventy-two hours and placed her back in the witch's arms. Ibrahim picked up a suitcase that Corrine must have packed.

"I'm going to go next door and distract Sofia," I said. "So that she doesn't see you leave without telling her. I don't know how she would react."

Corrine nodded and I left for Sofia's bedroom. Nothing could have prepared me for what I saw.

An empty bed.

"Sofia?"

I ducked down beneath the bed to check she wasn't hiding. I ripped open the cupboards. Then I dashed back out and checked every other room in the hut, yelling out her name as I did.

She wasn't in the building.

Would she be so mad as to leave for Headquarters in broad daylight? How does she even plan to get there?

Panic gripped me as I ran outside onto the terrace. It was still morning but the sun was already beating down, the heat rising by the second.

She could die out there.

Chapter 10: Sofia

Soon after Derek left the room, I found myself jumping out of the window and landing on the hot sand below. The moment the sun's rays came in direct contact with my skin, my whole body erupted in agony. It felt like someone had poured gasoline over me and lit me on fire.

What is the Elder thinking? Is it trying to murder me?

Despite the torture, my legs moved quickly, rushing across the beach toward Liana and the submarine. I ran for several minutes, and just as it felt like my skin was starting to peel away, I dove into the ocean. The water cooled my skin and gave me some relief, but the sunlight was still trickling down on me through the waves.

Fortunately, I didn't have to wait long before the submarine came into view. I swam deeper and knocked on the hatch. A few moments later, it surfaced and bobbed up above the waves. I swam up and grabbed onto the side of the black vessel, hoisting myself up and exposing myself once again to the full heat of the day. I quickly climbed into the hatch and closed the door behind me.

Once inside, I sank into a corner. Liana frowned as she eyed my body.

"Your vessel's in terrible shape."

Christ, if you wanted to leave, couldn't you have waited a few more hours until nightfall? I shouted at the Elder. *This is my body you're wrecking.*

Liana took a small vial of blood from her cloak pocket and poured it into my mouth. "That should heal your wounds and stop the skin from peeling." Then she retreated to the control room. The submarine jolted downward and started picking up speed toward... I had no idea where.

It took only a few minutes for the blood—that of an immune, I assumed from its sweet taste—to work its magic. My skin stopped stinging and started to feel smooth and cold again.

Where are we going? Headquarters? I asked. My Elder remained silent.

I was glad that there was no mirror in the submarine; I probably would have frightened myself to death when I'd first entered. But despite the torture I'd just endured, I was immensely grateful to be leaving Derek and Rose. I recalled the hurt in Derek's eyes after my behavior. He'd be turning the hut upside down, looking for me, crying out my name, wondering why I'd left him. I knew he'd be worrying himself sick that I might have ventured out in broad daylight. I tried to suck in my emotions.

You're safe without me, my love. I can't hurt you while we're apart.

"Don't get too comfortable." My parasite finally broke the silence. "Your family hasn't seen the last of you."

I shuddered internally but decided to change the subject. I finally dared to ask the question that had been recurring in my mind ever since I woke up in Cruor.

I'm supposed to be an immune. How did you turn me? Why am I a vampire?

There was a long pause, but the Elder answered me, perhaps out of boredom. "Indeed, you were an immune. In this human realm, no vampire could turn you. But once an immune is brought to our realm… well, Cruor has a way of breaking down that immunity."

I recalled the atmosphere of that place. I could easily believe what the Elder was telling me; it had certainly felt toxic, infectious. I wondered whether there was any cure for a vampire born out of Cruor. Whether—if I ever managed to break free from the Elder's clutches—there was any hope of living a normal life.

My body quivered again.

Why do you want to go to Headquarters so much? I asked, eager to divert my attention away from my fate.

"You'll find out soon enough."

Why did we leave the hut so suddenly?

"I don't have patience to argue with that fool. A period of absence should make him more malleable. But, fear not, we have things to do in the meantime to keep you occupied."

The words sent shivers running through me. But more than my own safety, I feared for my husband's.

You have my memories; it's not like you don't know the location of Hawk Headquarters. Why do you need Derek to escort us there?

"He'll serve as an extra layer of protection for you as my vessel, and consequently myself. You'll understand how this will prove to be valuable once we arrive and begin our mission. There aren't many people who will risk their life for you to the extent that he will."

Chapter 11: Derek

Corrine stood by the front door, clutching Rose in her arms, and Ibrahim stood next to her. They watched as I ripped through the small hut for the third time. I was in denial, refusing to accept that I had lost Sofia yet again.

Finally, I slumped down in a chair and admitted defeat. *What a pathetic husband you are. Your wife miraculously returned to you and you couldn't even keep hold of her for more than a few hours.*

I looked up at Corrine and Ibrahim and shook my head. "She's gone," I croaked.

"What on earth could have possessed her to leave in broad daylight?" Corrine's face contorted with distress.

"I just don't understand. She was insisting on visiting Headquarters. I argued with her, but how on earth could she think she'd be able to travel there with the sun shining? I can't believe she would be that stupid."

"Maybe she's just lost her mind," Ibrahim said.

"What if the Ageless took her?" The idea hit me like a punch in the gut.

"I would have sensed her. I doubt very much that the Ageless is behind this."

"Then where is she?" I smashed my fist down against the coffee table and it shattered, shards of glass cutting into my hand. I barely noticed the pain. If anything it distracted me from the anguish that was eating me away inside. The carpet started to singe beneath my feat. My body was heating up rapidly.

"Leave with Rose. Leave now! Before I burn you all to ashes."

Corrine exited the hut with the baby, but Ibrahim stayed behind and stepped toward me. "Do you need my assistance?"

"No. Just leave. I need to practice controlling my own power."

"Will you follow us to the new house?"

"Not until I've found Sofia. I can't leave this location in case she returns. Now, enough talk. Just leave with Corrine."

Ibrahim gave in to my request and followed Corrine through the door.

Now alone, I jumped over the terrace and dug my feet into the sand. Its heat melded with my own as I ran along the beach. I ran along the shore for miles, first in one direction, then in the other. I'd been half expecting to find Sofia lying in a heap unconscious somewhere along that coast. But I didn't.

Then I made my way to the nearby village, thinking that perhaps Sofia had got it into her head to meet Corrine's friends, whom I'd mentioned to her in passing. I stopped by their house and was lucky enough that they understood some English, for I spoke no Spanish. They hadn't seen any pale redhead pass their way.

One of them was kind enough to accompany me to the local market and ask around for Sofia. But nobody had seen her.

By the time I had finished my search, darkness had fallen and it was well past midnight. I returned to the hut with a sinking feeling in my stomach. *How am I going to tell Aiden?*

I picked up my phone and dialed the number for the main switchboard at Headquarters.

"I need to speak to Aiden Claremont."

"He's retired to his rooms now, sir. I doubt he's still awake. Can I take a message?"

"No. Go to his apartment and wake him up immediately. Tell him Derek Novak is on the phone."

Soon enough, Aiden's groggy voice was on the other end of the line.

"Derek? What's going on? Are you ready for me to send an aircraft to collect the two of you?"

"Aiden, Sofia's gone."

"Huh? What? I thought she returned."

"Yes, she did. But then she disappeared again. I'll explain everything, but first, I think there's a small chance she's headed for Headquarters. You need to watch out for her arrival and bring her into your custody. Don't alert everyone there—especially not Arron. Only warn the people you trust."

"Why?"

"Because she… she's now a vampire."

"Wh-what! Derek, have you lost your mind? How is that possible?"

"I don't know. She claimed she didn't know herself."

Aiden asked me a barrage of further questions about the details of Sofia's escape from Cruor, her arrival at the hut, and the short time I'd spent with her. I told him everything I knew, except for the strange change in her personality. I didn't have the heart to tell Aiden yet. The poor man was barely coping with the bad news that I'd just given him.

"So then what happened when she left and why do you think she's headed here?" Aiden asked.

"She was insistent on coming to headquarters. We'd just been discussing it before I left the room to speak to Corrine. When I returned, she had vanished."

There was a pause. Then Aiden cleared his throat and said, "I'll alert people at once. What are you going to do?"

"I have no choice but to stay here until she's found. I've been out all day searching the area, but now I need to stay put. There's always a chance she could return here looking for me."

"What about Rose?"

"She left with Corrine and Ibrahim to a new location. Now, can you please put me on the line to Vivienne? I need to speak to her."

Another fifteen minutes passed before I heard Vivienne's voice in my ear.

"Derek? What's happening?"

I relayed everything I'd just told Aiden. I went further and told her about the changes I'd observed in Sofia's behavior. Then I described to her my recurring nightmares.

"Derek, I... I know you want to draw some kind of comfort from me. And I didn't want to say anything because you're already under enough stress, but..."

"But what?"

"Recently I've been having visions of my own... visions that are almost identical to those you've just described."

As twins, Vivienne and I having the same visions didn't happen often. But when it did occur, it was never a good thing.

Chapter 12: Sofia

The submarine eventually stopped moving. When I poked my head through the hatch and realized we were back at The Shade's port, I felt bewildered. *Why are we back here?* I climbed out and headed for the forest. After hurrying through the trees for several minutes, I reached the foot of one of the large mountains bordering the island. My hands gripped the sharp rocks and I began to climb until I found myself at the entrance of a large cave that I'd never seen before throughout my time at The Shade.

My legs walked me inside and the Elder spoke. "Don't even think about moving from here."

What? How can I when...

All of a sudden, the ice within my bones started to melt. The heaviness in my body began to lift. The Elder's suffocating presence was leaving me. My breathing relaxed as I found myself able to move again.

But then a wave of exhaustion hit me and my legs gave way

beneath me. I lay down on the damp cave floor. My eyelids drooped. My muscles felt like they'd just endured a thousand-mile run. My joints ached. My entire body begged for sleep.

Just as I was about to drift off, someone called my name. The voice was strangely familiar. I managed to open my eyes and a figure moved out from behind the shadows at the back of the cave. Ashley. She helped me into a sitting position, leaning my back against the wall.

"Oh my God, how have you been?" I asked, staring at her face, relieved to see that she displayed no symptoms of being inhabited by an Elder. Assuming she hadn't had the same special treatment as me, this was Ashley in her true state. Her eyes looked red and puffy and her skin had a slight grey tinge to it. She looked distraught and barely managed a smile on seeing me.

"I-I killed him."

"Who?"

"S-Sam. I-I killed Sam."

"What are you saying, Ashley?"

"The Elders. Th-they made me do it." She started shaking violently and broke down sobbing against my chest.

I put my arms around her and kissed her head. What could I say? No words could console her. So I remained silent, tears of my own welling in my eyes. I held her in my arms, brushing through her hair with my hand and rocking gently from side to side. Although my body was groaning for sleep, Ashley was in desperate need of me.

After what seemed like hours, her voice had grown hoarse and she stopped crying. She looked exhausted as she lifted her eyes up to me and kissed my cheek.

"Thank you for being here for me."

I nodded, still lost for words over her tragedy.

"I've been all alone," she continued. "My Elder really put me through a lot when it was inhabiting me. I guess it didn't want to use me up all at once and have me expire, so it brought me here and told me to rest until it returned."

"Expire," I murmured. "Is that what happened to Xavier?"

"I don't know. I haven't seen him for days. What I do know is that Elders can only inhabit our bodies for a certain amount of time. Giving us breaks allows us to last longer, but eventually we will die." The tone of Ashley's voice was strangely calm. There was no sign of fight left in her.

Ashley paused before asking, "Why do you think Xavier expired?"

I told her about my visit to Cruor and how the Elder inhabiting Xavier had transferred to me. I now feared the worst for him and my heart sank for Vivienne. She had sacrificed so much for Derek and I, for her family, for The Shade. She deserved to finally live a life of her own and we all knew that she loved Xavier deeply. I had been hoping that she'd allow him into her life. Now she might be denied that chance forever.

Ashley interrupted my mourning. "Sofia, how did they turn you? I thought you were immune to the curse."

"They brought me to Cruor. Apparently, the atmosphere there can break down immunity. I assume one of their vessels bit me while I was still unconscious." I traced my neck, feeling for the bite marks. Sure enough, there were two small bumps at the base of my neck.

"I wonder how it works," I continued. "If these creatures known as Elders are the original form of vampire, how did they start creating human mutations of themselves? How were they even able to infect humans with vampirism when they seem to have no physical form?"

"From what I've gathered, the original 'vessels', or human vampires, were created a long, long time ago simply by being kept in

Cruor long enough. The darkness of that place manifested itself physically. Once infected, those human vampires could then turn others by biting them and inserting their venom directly into their bloodstream. We vessels are valuable to them because the only way the Elders can enjoy the pleasures of a physical form is by inhabiting one of us. They can't directly inhabit a human's body. The human first needs to be infected with their dark nature."

My head spun with all this new and disturbing information.

"How did they manage to get to Earth in the first place? What is it with all these gates? Who created them?"

"I don't know much else about their history, Sofia. My Elder wasn't exactly open to questions. What I do know is that the vast majority of humans and vampires who didn't escape The Shade are now locked up in The Cells. The Elders have started gathering up dozens of vampires and taking them out on expeditions. I've been on one already and it was…" Ashley stopped herself mid-sentence.

"What? Tell me about these expeditions." When she remained silent, I shook her a little. "Tell me!"

"No, Sofia, I don't want to talk about it. I don't want to disturb you any more than I already have because we both need to try to get some sleep now. Our bodies will need it."

Chapter 13: Sofia

I woke up to something cold nestling against me. For a moment I thought it was Ashley, but when I opened my eyes, I found myself staring at Abby. She'd lain down so that her head was level with mine.

"Abby!" I exclaimed, drawing her closer to me and kissing her forehead. "Oh, thank heavens you're not still stuck in that dreadful place. Are you okay, darling?"

"Sofia, I'm really hungry. Why did they want to make me a vampire?"

"Abby, I-I don't know." I couldn't think of an answer that wouldn't scare her senseless.

"I'm so hungry. And they said I can't have the tasty blood. They keep giving me the bitter one, so I spit it out. Then they hurt me and tell me not to waste it and…"

"What did they do to you?"

"They hit my back real hard. But it doesn't hurt any more because they gave me some medicine. Also sometimes I feel so cold and I can't breathe properly. I think of that poltergeist movie Ben showed me once and it feels like that, like a ghost is inside me. I'm scared that it's going to happen again."

Abby began to whimper. I didn't want her to see the tears falling from my own eyes so I just buried her face beneath my chin and hugged her. After a few minutes she stopped crying and said something that chilled me to the bone.

"Sofia, why did you kill my mom?"

"Huh? What are you saying, Abby? I never…"

"Don't lie. I saw you. You ripped out her heart. Why did you kill my mom?"

She thinks Clara was her mother. Abby lifted her head up to face me. Her irises had turned black. She stood up.

"Why are you ignoring my question, Sofia?"

Claws appeared from her hands and, without warning, she launched herself toward my chest. I managed to catch her hands just before they dug deep.

"Stop! Abby, stop it!"

"You tore out my mommy's heart. Now I'll tear out yours."

I managed to scramble to my feet so I could take advantage of my height. Unable to reach me, she sank her teeth deep into my right arm. The pain caused me to lose my grip on her. She positioned herself on a high rock and was about to jump on me again when Ashley appeared behind her, grabbing her by the waist and hurling her to the ground against the sharp stone floor.

But this barely deterred Abby. She got up and this time turned on Ashley. Letting out a shriek, she climbed up the rock and grabbed Ashley's foot, making Ashley tumble to the ground. Abby followed her down and, with her claws still bared, was about to tear through

Ashley's throat when a chilling breeze entered the cave.

Abby let out a small scream and halted mid-motion. Her eyes turned translucent and her mouth hung open awkwardly. Then she stepped back and made her way toward the exit of the cave. As she left, her own voice said:

"You need to control yourself, little girl. We can't have you spoiling perfectly capable vessels."

Abby left the cave and sped down the mountain. "Where do you think it's taking her?" I gasped.

"To be locked up with the others, I guess. That one's feisty." Ashley was still catching her breath.

I stood rooted to the spot, stunned. *My sweet little Abby. Where has she gone?* I thought about my best friend, Ben. And then his parents. They had lost their lives because of their connection to me. *I can't let that happen to Abby.*

I hadn't noticed a second cold breeze enter the cave until Ashley let out a cry. Her body contorted before she stood upright. Her eyes were still clear though and her face looked normal; I assumed she must have paid a visit to the witch in The Cells like I had.

"I've given you enough rest. Now we have work to do." She walked toward the exit and began to climb down the mountain.

"Wait!" I ran after her. "Where are you going?"

As if to answer me, another cold breeze blew through the cave, but this time it settled within my own bones.

"You'll see." My mouth spoke.

I climbed down the mountain after Ashley and followed her back toward the direction of the Port. On arrival, we were met with a dozen vampires huddled together and talking with each other—all of them female. Many of them had familiar faces; they were residents of The Shade, but most of them I had never spoken to. Each of them had a normal appearance like Ashley and I, but it was clear from their conversations that they too were possessed.

A beautiful young vampire with black hair walked up to Ashley and I, handing us two short cocktail dresses. "Put these on. We're leaving in a moment."

Everyone else was wearing the same type of clothing, the type one would wear on a night out or to a party. Without considering modesty, Ashley and I stripped and quickly pulled the new garments over our bodies.

What on earth are we doing?

My voice spoke up above the chattering.

"Are we ready?"

"Yes," they replied in unison.

My head turned toward a large submarine that had just surfaced. It was the biggest I'd seen of The Shade's fleet. It looked capable of carrying at least a hundred people. The hatch opened and we began to pile in. I was the last to enter. I closed the hatch behind me and climbed down the metal ladder. While Ashley and the others took seats in the main passenger area, I headed directly to a small room at the front of the ship, where I found Liana sitting in the captain's seat behind all the main controls. Once again, it seemed like she would be forced to navigate the submarine to wherever we were headed.

"I need another vial." I held out my right arm to show Liana where Abby had bitten me. I had almost forgotten about the wound. She reached into her cloak and withdrew another one. I gulped down the sweet blood and within a few moments I had healed.

I sat down in a chair next to Liana. She started moving switches and punching in coordinates. Then she took hold of the wheel and we jolted forward. Her eyes were still translucent, yet I knew that she must now be in control of her actions for her to be navigating the submarine. It must have been a struggle to control such a large piece of machinery with impaired vision, but she was managing it somehow.

There wasn't much to look at as I sat there. We sped through the occasional school of fish, but for the most part, we were travelling too fast to see anything other than the dark expanse of water stretched out in front of us. We had now travelled far past the boundary of The Shade, so I assumed that it must be nighttime.

Apprehension filled me as Liana began slowing the vessel and we started rising. As soon as we entered shallower waters, I got up and made my way into the passenger area.

"Come on, ladies." A smirk formed on my mouth. "It's time."

I was the first to climb up the ladder and push open the hatch. The air was warm and booming music filled my ears. Although we'd parked on a dark stretch of empty beach, multi-colored disco lights flashed less than a mile away. Crowds of people danced and shouted.

It didn't take much guessing to know what we were here for. *They sure have instincts for what makes for an easy target. Intoxicated young men at a beach rave. At nighttime. They won't even realize we're vampires.*

We hurried out of the water and onto the beach, heading toward the lights. As we got nearer, men started to notice us and wolf-whistle. I cringed as I imagined what we looked like: a large group of pretty young women in dresses that barely covered our backsides, all dashing toward them at once.

We reached the crowd and each headed for the first man who caught our eye. For me, that happened to be a short round fellow with hair down to his shoulders. He looked like he was in his early twenties. *Poor guy. Doesn't know what he's getting himself into.*

"Hello," I said, walking up to him and fluttering my eyelashes.

"Hi, I'm Jason." His face was bright red and he held a nearly-finished can of beer in one hand.

"I'm… Ava. Ooof, it's so hot here. Do you want to come for a walk with me?"

The man stuttered and looked at me like he was physically incapable of refusing. "Oh, s-sure, Ava. That's such a cool name, by the way. I just need to let Matthew know… it's his party, ya see. I'm his best man!"

A bachelor party. This is worse than I thought.

He rushed over to Matthew, whispered something in his ear, and sped back toward me with a huge grin on his chubby face. He looked like he'd just hit the jackpot. I took his hand, placed it around my waist, and led him away from all the noise and smoke.

"I want to take you somewhere special," I purred.

"Oh, do ya? Where might that be?"

"You'll see. Let's run."

Once we were far enough away for his screams to be inaudible beneath the loud music, I pulled his head toward me and bit into his neck, inserting my venom. He squealed and struggled at first, trying to escape my grip, but eventually his body became too weak and he fell to the ground, twitching. I picked him up and flung him over my shoulder like he was a sack of coal. Within a few seconds, I was by the open hatch to the submarine. Liana reached out her hands and I handed the man to her. Then I washed my mouth in the sea, removing all traces of blood from my face, and headed back to the party.

I caught a few more men in this way, some tall, short, skinny and round. The Elder didn't seem to have any particular preference. It went for whoever was the easiest target. I even managed to lure away a drunk girl by telling her I had some bottles of free booze and needed her help carrying them.

As I travelled back and forth from the submarine, I passed by other vampires with their victims. Once we'd finished with the bachelor party, we quickly moved further down the beach and started work on another party. It turned out that the beach was lined with dozens of late-night raves.

We finished our work only when Liana indicated that we couldn't fit any more people in the submarine, at which point we all returned through the hatch. I gasped to see the yield of our fishing expedition. The floor of the passenger area was lined with people writhing and screaming, most still in the middle of their transformation.

What have I just done? I looked around at Ashley and the other female vessels, my accomplices. Behind their hollow eyes, I knew they all felt the same.

Sensing my horror, a voice hissed in my ear.

Won't you be proud of your little Rose helping us do this one day...

CHAPTER 14: DEREK

Days had passed and Sofia had still not returned. Being cooped up in that little cabin, listening to the seconds tick by, was beginning to drive me insane.

I'd been on the phone to Aiden three times a day since her disappearance. He had no news for me either. It was a mystery. We were back to square one, only this time, we didn't even have any clue as to her location. No matter how hopeless the situation had been before, at least we'd known from the Ageless that she'd been sent to Cruor. Aiden suspected that the witch had come for her again. What other explanation could there be?

A voice began to nag at me, a voice that I'd been trying to exile. *If, as Ibrahim suggested, Sofia had indeed lost her mind, she could have run out in the sun and committed suicide. Maybe you just didn't spot the body...*

I picked up my phone and dialed Corrine's number.

"Derek? Have you found her?" Corrine answered the phone.

"No, Corrine. But I need to speak to Ibrahim right away."

I heard Corrine calling for him and he came on the line a few seconds later.

"Sofia still hasn't returned," I said. "And she hasn't arrived at Headquarters either. I think you were wrong about the Ageless. She *must* have come for her again. It's the only thing that makes sense."

"Derek, I've communicated with the Ageless. She didn't come for your wife again."

"Then she's lying!" I shouted, punching my fist through a cupboard door.

"I'm not lying, Derek." A cool voice spoke from behind me.

I dropped the phone. Whirling around, I found myself face to face with the witch who'd stolen my life from me. Fury boiled within me on seeing her standing there, so calm and collected. It took all my willpower to not lunge for her throat.

"You!" I spat. "What made you deign to appear now?"

"You haven't been cooperating," she said bluntly. "You've neglected your mission of gathering up immunes and helping restore balance."

Is she insane?

The insolent tone of her voice made me lose all control. A blaze of fire shot from my palms and flew right toward the witch. It set the end of her long silver robe alight. She mumbled a few words and water gushed out of her own palms, extinguishing the fire.

My chest still heaving with outrage, I tried to steady the shaking in my voice as I said, "Listen, you bitch. If you wish to continue standing there with that long hair of yours intact, you'd better rethink your attitude."

"I thought that you had understood the importance of maintaining balance between…"

"Balance! Pray tell, exactly what is this 'balance', witch? Because I haven't seen any semblance of *balance* here. Now that I think about it, the only *balance* I've witnessed is in your heavenly realm. Is that just a coincidence?" Fire reignited from my palms, forcing her to douse the cabin with water.

This time, to my surprise, the witch cast her head downward. I'd hardly ever seen her face express emotions. But I could have sworn that I saw a flicker of guilt.

Finally she cleared her throat. "We had never intended for things to get this out of hand."

"What are you talking about?"

The witch sighed and took a seat in a chair. She motioned that I do the same.

The Ageless leaned forward and spoke in a low voice. "What I'm about to tell you has never been revealed to anyone from this realm before. It's part of our kind's ancient history. But first, close your eyes." When I looked at her untrustingly, the only reassurance she gave me was: "You'll understand why soon enough."

I didn't trust her, but I was so hungry to hear what she had to say, I decided not to argue. As soon as I shut my eyes, a strange vision appeared in my mind. I was looking down upon a vast range of black mountains that stretched out as far as I could see. There was not a hint of vegetation in sight, nor any other life for that matter, just miles upon miles of shades of black and grey. There appeared to be no sun, yet the sky, which was speckled with dark clouds, had an eerie reddish tinge.

"Where on Earth…?" I began to ask.

"Not Earth," the Ageless said. "That is Cruor, a dead realm. It's devoid of life, save for the hapless souls that have been kidnapped there. The Elders live like spirits within the bowels of the mountains."

"What kind of evil are these creatures?"

"They have no physical form of their own. They are like parasites. Their very existence depends upon sucking life out of others. Blood is of particular value to them. They store blood and—even when they are not inhabiting a vessel and thus cannot drink it—they gain sustenance from it simply by remaining in close proximity. The blood of immunes is particularly potent…"

"Immunes," I said suddenly. "How is Sofia a vampire?"

"Immunes on Earth are no longer immunes once brought to Cruor. They become too affected by the atmosphere of that realm to resist infection."

"What *are* immunes? How did they come to be?" I opened my eyes briefly to see the witch shift in her chair.

"That is a long story… Close your eyes again." This time the vision of a very different realm appeared. "Behold, Aviary, realm of the Hawks, or 'Guardians' as they like to call themselves."

A harsh sun beat down on dense jungles. I'd always thought that our redwoods at The Shade were magnificent, but the trees of Aviary were three times the width. Swarms of bees the size of small birds buzzed around giant flowers. The place seemed larger than life, almost Jurassic. Wild four-legged carnivores the likes of which I'd never encountered before raced through the vegetation. Massive predatory birds crowded the skies. Finally, I spotted the Hawks themselves, muscular men and women whose features would have looked almost human, had it not been for their sharp beaks and black wings. I recognized them from when Arron had arranged for some to accompany us during the storming of The Blood Keep.

"Cruor and Aviary," the witch continued, "have been enemies since time immemorial. Legend has it that the Elders of Cruor attacked Aviary to extract its life source. And the Hawks… well, they don't forgive easily. They've been at war with Cruor ever since."

"All right. But you still haven't answered my question. What are immunes?" I said.

"There was a time, before I came to power, when Cruor posed its first threat to The Sanctuary. We… we didn't want this looming over us. We struck a bargain with the Elders that we'd provide them with access to sustenance and in return they would leave us in peace. My ancestors used their magic to create gates between the vampire realm and Earth. To make the deal more attractive for the Elders, we also created 'immunes'. We arrived at a potion that could be injected into a human's bloodstream. It made their blood sweeter, but most of all, they were immune to being turned into vampires while on Earth. Their succulent blood could be consumed without fear of turning them. We created only a few thousand immunes, but with time those blood strands were passed on through the generations."

My mind was beginning to reel at the sheer scope of the witches' deception. Perhaps sensing my rage, the witch moved on. "So… now that we had pacified the Elders, we thought our problems had been solved. That was until Aviary turned on us and threatened to storm our realm for assisting their enemies. In their eyes, we had given Cruor an unfair advantage. Thus, to pacify the Hawks, we agreed to create their own gates to Earth, in order to maintain a balance between the two realms."

At this point, I could no longer contain my anger. "Why the hell did you have to divert all this to us? Couldn't you just have destroyed the gates linking to your own realm, the gates between The Sanctuary and Cruor and Aviary?"

"Between the supernatural realms, no gates are needed. It's only when entering this mortal realm that we require special portals." The witch continued as if I hadn't interrupted. "Maintaining a balance has always been challenging, since one realm was always trying to gain more of a foothold than the other. But, since your discovery of the cure to vampirism and the arrival of numerous Elders, we've been forced to implicate your kind more and more in this struggle…"

"So let me get this clear," I fumed. My palms felt like they were about to start blazing again. "This balance you've been harping on about is nothing but a way to save your own backsides from getting burned. Everything revolves around diverting the heat away from your realm toward ours. You stole my wife from me because Cruor demanded it and you were too scared to deny them. And to top it all off, you had the gall to try to persuade me to help you with all of this by collecting immunes for you!" I spat at her feet. "You're nothing but conceited self-serving cowards. You don't deserve the air you breathe." I directed my palms to her and more flames erupted.

The witch's eyes widened before she once again manifested water to extinguish my fire. "If you were in our position, wouldn't you have done the same to protect your own kind?"

"Deliberately direct such evil toward vulnerable people who'd never done my kind any harm? Do you really need me to answer that?" I stormed out onto the verandah. "And why are you even here telling me all of this? Out of the goodness of your heart?" I sneered at her.

The witch followed me outside. "You must understand that my role as leader has always been to follow in the footsteps of my ancestors, the Ancients. For the protection of our kind, they set down rules that I and my council have always abided by… but Ibrahim has opened my mind to another possibility."

"Oh, and what is that?"

"Working together might serve our realm better."

"Again, *your* realm! *Your* safety. *Your* peace of mind. Let's ignore the countless innocent lives you've ripped apart and the many more you're about to destroy. Can we please spend more time thinking about how we can keep you comfortable? Because I honestly don't think enough effort has been put into that already."

It was hard to find words to express my exasperation and disbelief. I stared at her, struggling to comprehend that any creature could be so incapable of conscience. I recalled the flash of guilt in her eyes. *Is this just an act she is forced to put on to retain her status as leader to her kind? Or perhaps that look of guilt was meant to manipulate me, and the inhabitants of The Sanctuary do indeed have hearts of stone... or no hearts at all.*

"Our realm is called 'The Sanctuary' for a reason," she said coolly. "As leader, I must abide by our code which is, first and foremost, to ensure the serenity of our kind."

My eyes narrowed. "So, given that you are the only beings in the universe whose existence matters, why would you want to risk upsetting your balance? You seem to be managing just fine. Why do you even want our cooperation?"

"Since the discovery of the cure—something even I didn't foresee—and the influx of Elders through the portal, tension between the Elders and Hawks has been growing rapidly. Each side is becoming more and more demanding and it's becoming impossible to satisfy them. Recent demands that we could not reconcile have led to direct threats to our own realm, something that hasn't happened since I began my rule."

"I see," I said. "Now that using us as your pawns has become troublesome for *you*, you've realized that removing us as bait from the table is going to make life easier for *you*... because?"

"They won't have as much to fight over. If we seal off their entries into this realm then, yes, their attention will be on us. But that is already starting to happen. When you're drifting in a sea of sharks, having two sacks of raw meat will produce more of a signal for attack than having just one."

I nodded slowly. At least the witch now seemed to have decided to be honest with me about the level of their narcissism. "If you want cooperation, first tell me where my wife is."

"I don't know that we want cooperation yet," she said. "I must call a meeting back in my realm with my council. Until I've done this, I can't reveal anything to you about Sofia. That would be a signal to the Elders that we are no longer neutral." Then she paused and looked intensely into my eyes. "But I will call this council, Derek. You have my word. And if this plan meets with approval, I will return to you."

Before I could open my mouth, she had vanished just as suddenly as she had appeared.

"Curse you!" I yelled, stamping my foot. *Sofia could be dead by the time you've finished with your damn meeting.* I climbed off the terrace and ran to the ocean. When I dove in, my body hissed like a hot pan splashed with water.

I floated on my back and reflected on the witch's proposal. Even if the council agreed that it was indeed in their best interest to eliminate the portals, how did I know that, once the Elders and Guardians had been banished, the witches wouldn't have some other hidden agenda for us?

When you're drowning and all you're handed is the end of a sword to pull you up above the waves, do you take it?

But at that moment, I had no idea whether the witch would keep her word to call a meeting. And even if she did, how long would that take? Every second that went by was a second that Sofia could be suffering somewhere, in need of rescue. What aggravated me most was the fact that the witch hadn't denied knowing where Sofia was. My gut instinct told me that she knew very well what had happened to Sofia during her initial time in Cruor, and why Sofia had been taken again. Yet the witch refused to give me even that much relief. *After everything she's done.*

What am I to do in the meantime? I floated for hours. But once the sun had ducked beneath the horizon, I decided that there was simply no way I could stay in that place any longer. I'd be of far more use travelling back to Headquarters and working with Aiden. I'd leave a note for Sofia telling her where I'd gone and I'd travel back to the cabin every two days to check if she had returned.

On arriving at my bedroom, it turned out that leaving a note wasn't necessary. For there lay Sofia, sprawled unconscious on the bed, her skin covered with blisters and blood seeping from a deep wound near her abdomen.

Chapter 15: Sofia

As the blackness gave way to fluorescent white lighting, the first thing that came into focus was a set of bright blue eyes. A warm hand brushed against my cheek. *Derek.* Relief overwhelmed me, but as I came further to consciousness and realized what a danger I was to my loved ones, it transformed into horror.

Derek's face lit up as soon as I stirred. He bent down and his lips pushed against mine. I wished I could have returned his embrace with as much passion. Instead my lips and arms remained stiff. The Elder retained full control of my movements.

"Sofia!" my father gasped.

Oh, no. Not you too.

I turned my head to see Aiden on the other side of my bed. He clutched my hand, leant down and kissed my forehead. Pain was etched in his eyes. He'd already lost his wife to the curse. Now he was watching me suffer under it. *Thank God he doesn't know my situation is even worse than Ingrid's was. I don't know how he would survive it.*

"You're going to be okay, my darling," Aiden said. "We're going to find a cure for you, just as we did for Derek. And then we're going to bring your beautiful baby boy back to your arms. How does that sound?"

I was desperate to ask about my son, but my lips remained tightly sealed. I looked around for the first time. We were in the emergency room at Hawk Headquarters.

Why does it want me here?

A nurse walked over to me and helped me into a sitting position. It was then that the remains of a mouthful of blood trickled down to the base of my tongue. *Sweet. Succulent.*

"You're lucky we retained some of Anna's blood from the lab when we were doing tests on her." The nurse smiled.

Anna's blood. Although I couldn't deny my craving for more, I felt disgusted. *Whatever did happen to Anna? And what about Kyle who accompanied her here all those months ago, just after he became a human?*

Aiden must have guessed such questions would have been running through my mind. "Anna and Kyle are okay, Sofia. They're in Aviary right now. Arron brought Ian there too. But they will be returned unharmed. They are just assisting the Guardians with some testing."

Aviary? Guardians? Testing? I had no idea what he was talking about, but none of it put me at ease for my friends' safety.

His face betrayed realization that he'd implicated himself in a longer and more complicated discussion than he had intended. "But all that, my dear, is a topic for another day. We need to get you better first."

"How long before I can leave this bed?"

"Immediately," the nurse said. "Take a look, you're all healed."

The blisters and all traces of my wound had vanished. I shivered internally as I recalled my trip to the witch in The Cells who, in exchange for some more dried bread, had carved the wound into my body and covered my skin with blisters as soon as we had returned from our… expedition.

"Where did you go, Sofia?" Derek must have been burning to ask.

"I-I don't know, Derek." I felt myself frown. "The last thing I remember was you leaving me in the bedroom. I was upset that you were refusing to bring me to see everyone here at Headquarters… I probably ran outside into the daylight. I suppose I worked myself up into a state and didn't know what I was doing. But I think that what we can learn from this is: don't make me upset again and I won't go anywhere."

Disappointment shrouded his eyes. He knew this wasn't his Sofia he was talking to. He wanted me back. *I* wanted me back.

"How did you get back to the cabin?" he pressed.

How did I get there?

The truthful answer was that I didn't know myself. After creating my wound, the witch had put me into unconsciousness and after that I remembered nothing. I guessed that Liana and her submarines must have had something to do with my journey.

"Again, I don't remember anything. My guess is that some humans from the local village spotted me and brought me there."

Derek was about to interrogate me further, but Aiden came to the Elder's rescue and interrupted him. "There'll be time for more questions later, Derek. Sofia has been through an ordeal and, although her body is looking better now, she clearly still needs some mental rest."

"Rest is exactly what I need. Thank you." I put my arms around my father's neck and kissed his cheek. Then I turned to speak to the nurse. "Where will I sleep?"

"What? With me in my quarters, of course." Derek didn't even give the woman a chance to answer. "I'm not letting you leave my sight after having you slip from my grasp twice already."

"No, D-Derek," I stuttered. "I c-can't sleep anywhere near you. I don't want to risk doing more harm to you than I've done already." I placed a hand underneath his shirt and traced my fingers over the scars I'd created on his torso. Then cold tears started to fall from my eyes. "P-please, I can't sleep anywhere near you."

Again my loving father came to the aid of the Elder. He gathered me in his arms and said, "Derek's not going to make you stay with him if you don't want that, honey. You can sleep wherever you want."

"No, she can't!" Derek hissed. "Aiden, are you mad? I am *not* going to let her out of my sight. Especially not during the long hours of the night. That's when she's most vulnerable! She needs supervision."

Aiden placed a hand on Derek's shoulder. "As long as she's within the boundaries of Headquarters, she'll be fine. I'll have security positioned at all exits to the main building during the day so she won't be able to go out into the sunlight, and around the outskirts of the entire grounds at night so she won't leave the campus even once it's dark. There was nothing stopping her leaving that little hut. You're forgetting that it's different here at Headquarters."

"I still don't trust…" Derek began, but Aiden cut him off.

"And," Aiden said in a low voice, "you know very well that there are other reasons why it's better that Sofia is kept away from everybody… why it's better that as few people as possible realize that she's back here."

At that, Derek remained silent. Then Aiden turned to me once again. "You can stay in whatever apartment you want while you're here, okay, darling?"

"Thank you, Dad," I piped up, giving him a cuddle. "I'd like to be in the quietest part of the building. I just feel that I need time alone to recover. I can move in with Derek when I'm ready."

Derek scowled, but he decided not to argue with Aiden in front of me. I was sure that a heated discussion would take place between the two men as soon as they were alone.

I hoped that Derek was now beyond taking my words and behavior seriously. I hoped that he simply accepted that I was deranged and needed some kind of psychiatric doctor. *Or do I dare hope that he might have guessed by now that I've been possessed?*

As the nurse guided me out of bed and set me on my feet, I felt relieved that this time, the Elder had decided to keep me apart from Derek. But a darker question entered my thoughts. The Elder had never had any qualms about hurting my husband before. Indeed, the Elder had willfully made me inflict suffering on him and I had felt the Elder shiver with pleasure.

Why does the Elder want to keep me completely isolated?

CHAPTER 16: SOFIA

Aiden took hold of my hand and led me out of the emergency room, Derek following behind us. In the hallway, I was met with a group of familiar faces: Vivienne, Cameron, Claudia, Gavin, Eli, Shadow and Landis.

"Sofia!" they exclaimed and rushed forward to greet me.

They all looked delighted to see me, except for Shadow. His first instinct was to arch his back and snarl. Eli tugged on his leash.

"Come on, boy. Stop that. Don't you remember your friend, Sofia?"

Shadow's snarls turned into barks, then whimpers. He dragged Eli away from me.

Eli glanced in Vivienne's direction. She too looked perturbed by Shadow's restlessness. Then Vivienne's eyes fell on me again.

Vivienne, if there's anyone in this place who can see through me, it's you. Please, Vivienne. Understand, I thought, hoping that she'd somehow read my mind.

Then I addressed the Elder directly. *Why do you want me apart from Derek? I thought you wanted him as protection?*

There may come a time when he will prove to be useful. But in the meantime, he's just an obstacle. And so are your other friends. We can't have anyone hampering our freedom of movement or monitoring you during the night, he replied to me silently.

Once the group had finished greeting me, Aiden said, "All right, guys, Sofia needs some rest. No doubt you'll have time to catch up later once she's feeling better."

Derek's hand found the small of my back as he walked on one side of me, with Aiden on the other. We made for the elevator and Aiden punched in the button for the top floor of the building. Once the door opened, we took a right turn and headed toward the very end of the long corridor. Despite staying at Headquarters for weeks at a time in the past, I'd never been to this part of the building before. We stopped in front of door number 721. Aiden pulled down on the handle and led us inside.

"Here you go, darling," Aiden said. "I hope everything is to your liking. This is one of the quietest apartments we have in Hawk Headquarters. Nobody will disturb you here."

I looked around the place briefly; there was a double bedroom with en suite bathroom, a kitchen area and a cozy sitting room. These living quarters were small compared to others that I'd seen in the building, but all the Elder cared about was its location.

"And where are your and Derek's apartments?" I asked Aiden.

"If you need me, I'm currently in room number 120 and Derek is number 219. Vivienne and your other friends are occupying rooms 340 to 346, in case you want to visit any of them. Don't worry, I'll write all this down on a piece of paper so you don't forget. And, of course, I'll be leaving you with the direct landline codes so you can call us whenever you want."

My father scribbled some numbers on a scrap of paper, which he slipped into a drawer. Then he pulled a phone out of his pocket and dialed a number. "Sarah, bring some goat blood up to room 721 as soon as you can." He hung up and looked at me again, pulling out two keys from his pocket and handing them to me. "Here's the key you should use whenever you leave the room. It locks the door from the outside. And this key you should use if you want to lock the door from the inside. Having two makes for better security. I'll put them in this drawer here. Okay, darling?"

I nodded and thanked him politely once again. But Aiden hadn't yet finished.

"Also, I'll leave you a spare key to my office as well as to my own apartment, so if you feel like it, you can go and hang around in either place in case I'm not there. And here's a spare key to Derek's apartment… So you've got plenty of places you can go to relax. I just need you to avoid all the main communal areas like the reception and training rooms."

Derek had remained silent the whole time. But his intense gaze bored into me. I didn't believe for a moment that he wouldn't still keep tabs on me.

"Okay, that's all clear," I heard myself say. "I'd like to be alone now. Please give me at least five days. I'll come find you when I'm ready." I walked to the door and held it open for them. "Thank you both for understanding."

Aiden walked out first, followed by Derek. I had almost closed the door when Derek's hand appeared through the crack. He pushed the door ajar just enough so that his face was visible.

"I'm going to find you again, Sofia." His look of determination sent chills running through me. Then he pulled the door shut and his footsteps disappeared down the hallway.

I just hope that it won't be too late, Derek.

I meandered over to the large French windows and opened them, sticking my head out and taking in the surroundings. Looking down at the ground made me feel nauseous. I doubted that even a vampire would survive that fall. The vineyards surrounding Headquarters stretched out for miles and, in the far distance, a towering wall enclosed the whole area.

Someone knocked at the door. I looked through the peephole before opening it. A middle-aged blonde hunter was standing outside, holding a large glass jug filled with blood.

"Here you go, dear," she said as I opened the door. "You should keep that in the fridge so it doesn't go stale."

I took the jug from her without even saying thank you and she left. I pried the lid off and drank directly from the container, blood spilling down the sides of my mouth. It tasted unbearably sour and I realized why vampires hated animal blood. Despite the taste, the Elder made me drink half of it in one go before placing it on a shelf in the fridge. I guessed that it wanted to make sure its *vessel* was nourished.

Now what? I asked in my head, as my body stretched itself out on the king-sized bed.

We wait until dark, the Elder replied.

CHAPTER 17: SOFIA

As each hour brought us closer to nightfall, I became more and more nervous about what the Elder was planning. I hoped more than anything that Derek wouldn't get in our way. I didn't know what the Elder would make me do to him should Derek obstruct its plans.

Once the clock had struck two am, I opened the drawer of my dressing table and took out the keys Aiden had left for me, save for those to the personal apartments of Derek and Aiden. I put them into my pocket and then headed for the front door. The doorknob didn't budge. I shook it, but it didn't move.

Your husband's doing, no doubt. He thought that sneaking back to lock you in at night would stop you roaming about. Never mind, there are other ways out of this room.

Dread filled me as we approached the large windows.

Have you lost your mind? I screamed at the Elder.

My parasite ignored me and drew open one of the windows. The sky was clear and a cool wind blew into the room. The full moon shone down over the landscape.

I found myself lifting one foot and placing it on the windowsill before hoisting my body up so that I was now inches away from a deadly fall. I braced myself as I anticipated the jump. I gripped the sides of the window frame and swung my legs out so that they now dangled down the side of the building. But, to my relief, instead of flinging myself to the ground, I lowered myself until my feet hit a metal pipe sticking out of the brick wall. I balanced precariously as my hands let go of the window. My heart raced as I wobbled, my bare feet almost losing my grip on the pipe.

Great move, monkey man. Christ. There's nothing else here I can grip on to...

With one powerful leap, I hurled myself sideways, toward the ledge of an adjacent window. But my hands slipped off the sill and I hurtled downward in a free fall. Just as I was bracing myself, my arms hit something and the next thing I knew, I was hanging from another metal pipe. I looked wildly around me. Just beneath my feet was another window that had been left ajar. My feet knocked against it and pushed it open. Then I swung my body through it and landed on my feet at the end of a quiet hallway.

I was still dizzy with shock and the last thing I wanted to do was race forward. But that was exactly what I found myself doing. I ran past countless doors and down dozens of staircases. I had no idea where the Elder was taking me. At one point I wondered whether he even had a destination in mind; he seemed to be taking me on a tour of the entire main building. But eventually we took a sharp left turn and ended up standing right outside Aiden's office. I entered the empty room.

I knelt on the floor and started rummaging through drawers and cupboards filled with documents. Noticing a key at the bottom of one of the cabinets, my hand reached down and put it into my pocket.

At least another hour passed by, and the Elder was still searching. Finally, as I got to work on the only drawers we hadn't touched, I uncovered a piece of yellowing paper with a map printed on it. A map of Headquarters. I hovered a finger over it for a couple of minutes before the Elder hissed in frustration.

This is not the map.

I tidied up all the papers and closed the drawers and cupboards until the room appeared to be back to its original state. Then I retreated out of the room and into the hallway, locking the door behind me.

I ran along half a dozen more corridors until I reached the reception area. Two male hunters sat on night duty behind the large desk. I approached them and my face split into a smile. I had never seen these men before, so I assumed that they were new and therefore didn't recognize me as Aiden's daughter. The lighting of the room was also dim, so it was possible that they hadn't even yet noticed that I was a vampire.

"Oh, don't mind me," I said to them. "I've just got insomnia so I'm having a bit of a walkabout. I wondered if you had a spare guest map and a phone sheet you could give me?"

One of them nodded and reached beneath his desk for two sheets of paper.

"Oh, and I'm just curious where the boss stays... you know, Arron?" I asked.

"Arron is in the detached building 'H', right at the bottom of the fields where the woods begin." The hunter picked up a pen and drew a black mark against the location for me. "But knowing that won't do you any good." He peered at me through his glasses. "Arron is an extremely busy man and when he does permit meetings, it's by appointment. His assistant's number is on the phone sheet."

"Oh, that's fine. Thank you."

I stuffed both pieces of paper into my pocket and walked away.

Arron... Why does the Elder want to seek out Arron?

It seemed that I wasn't about to get an answer as my legs headed back to my apartment. Thankfully, I'd packed the key to the exterior lock with me so we weren't forced to experiment any further with the Elder's skills as a gymnast.

On entering the apartment, I retrieved the map and the phone sheet from my pocket, unfolded them carefully, and placed them on the table next to the phone.

Now we wait once again, the Elder said.

Chapter 18: Sofia

Despite having fallen into a deep slumber after the night's escapades, I woke up feeling as if I hadn't slept at all. I looked at the alarm clock on my bedside: eleven am. As I turned in bed, I became aware of the ache that had returned to my muscles and joints. Realizing that the Elder had given me temporary control back over my movements, I took the opportunity to visit the bathroom and examine myself in front of the mirror.

My eyelids drooped. I tried to hold them wide open but they remained the same. Dark circles had developed under my eyes and my skin felt dehydrated. I splashed cold water on my face and grabbed some moisturizer from the cabinet, slathering it over myself.

Then sharp pangs in my stomach began to call on my attention and I walked to the fridge. Despite its taste, I chugged down the remainder of the animal blood. I was ravenous. I was about to attempt to call Aiden for more when a knock came at the door. Instantly, the Elder took back control and walked me to open it.

There stood Claudia, carrying two more large jugs of blood on a tray.

"Good morning." She smiled faintly before walking past me and putting the containers into my fridge. "I told Aiden I'd bring the blood to you." She walked toward me and grabbed hold of my shoulders. "I need to know what happened to Yuri." Her brown eyes blazed into mine.

"He didn't make it," my voice said. "His body was spoiled by the Elders. They made him fight to death with another vampire."

Claudia took in a sharp breath as though a hunter's bullet had just shot through her gut. Her eyes became unfocussed and her jaw fell open. Her knees buckled and she crumbled to the ground in a heap. I didn't help her. I just stood there, peering down at her now trembling form. The slight quivering in my own body didn't escape my notice, however.

I didn't know whether the Elder had deliberately told a lie just to get a thrill out of Claudia's reaction, or whether Yuri had indeed expired since I'd last seen him. Either way, my words had just ripped the blonde vampire apart.

I wanted to scoop the poor girl into my arms and hold her as I had done with Ashley. Instead, I walked over to the bedside table, picked up the phone sheet, and dialed the number to the emergency room.

"Hello, I'm calling from Room 721. There's someone here who needs your urgent assistance," I said, without even a hint of emotion in my voice.

"I'll send someone right over," a woman replied.

Urgent assistance. What Claudia needs is a friend's shoulder to cry on. Not someone prodding her on a sickbed.

A few minutes later, a nurse knocked on the door. She helped Claudia to her feet and guided her out of the room. I screamed at the

Elder within my head for an explanation, but all I got in response was stony silence.

Barely ten minutes had passed since they'd left when the Elder decided to make me leave the room myself. As we had done the night before, we ignored the elevators and headed straight for the staircases. We descended level after level until we arrived at the third floor. Then we walked along the corridor until we arrived outside of Room 340. I knocked loudly. Vivienne opened it.

"Sofia?" She looked surprised to see me. "Come in." She opened the door wide and beckoned me inside.

"Oh, no. I don't need to come in," I said. "I don't feel well, so I won't stay long at all, but I just thought I ought to tell you... Xavier's dead. His Elder used him up, then his body was thrown into a pit and ravaged by hounds."

No. No. No.

Vivienne clamped a hand over her mouth, stifling a gasp. She closed her eyes and her face scrunched up as if someone had just cut off her tongue. Then she staggered back into her apartment and slammed the door shut. But I still heard her break down. And as with Claudia, it seemed that with each sob that racked her body, my own limbs quivered, as if in rhythm.

I felt like I was about to collapse, but it seemed that the Elder wasn't yet finished with his fun.

Room 343.

Cameron emerged from the dark apartment. Like Vivienne, he displayed the same expression of mild shock upon seeing me.

"Sofia! How are you, my dear? You still look exhausted. Are you sure you should be wandering about? Do come in and have a seat."

"No, Cameron. Thanks for the invitation, but I'm fine, really," my voice said. "I just came to relay some news to you." I braced myself for the grenade that I knew was about to shatter him to pieces. "Liana. She's dead."

"Wh-what? What did you say?"

"The Elders killed her."

"No. It can't be." Cameron gripped the doorpost to steady himself, struggling to hold on to his denial.

"They possessed her for too long and made her weak. She was no longer of use to them so they drained her blood, then threw what was left of her into the sea for the sharks."

Cameron let out a wild howl, but his own choking silenced it. Next thing I knew, he was vomiting all over the floor. His knees buckled beneath him and he fell to the marble with a thud, stretched out in the middle of his doorway.

I left him that way. Alone in his suffering. My body once again finding pleasure in his wails.

A low snicker echoed in my ears.

Now that we've passed the time a little, we must return once again and rest until night time. I don't want to have to pay such a visit to your lover to inform him that you've expired... at least, not yet.

CHAPTER 19: SOFIA

As soon as all traces of daylight had vanished, I picked up the phone and dialed Arron's assistant.

"Hayden speaking," a female voice said. "Please state your name and how I can help."

"It's Aiden here."

The deep tone of my father's voice filled the bedroom. It took me a few seconds to realize that Aiden had indeed not suddenly entered the room, and that the male voice had emanated from my own mouth.

"I need Arron to meet me at Room 59. Tell him it's urgent."

"Well, it's getting late, but I'll see if I can still get through to him. Hold the line, please." She kept us waiting for only a few minutes before returning. "All right, he'll be at Room 59 in about ten minutes."

I hung up and rushed to the front door.

Locked again from the outside. Your lover continues to be diligent about his nighttime duties.

Dread filled the pit of my stomach as I hoisted myself out of the window once again and balanced myself on the metal pipe directly beneath me. It was only by some fluke that I'd survived last night's climb. *Can lightning strike twice?*

My body positioned itself to jump sideways toward the adjacent window. This time my hands latched onto the ledge and I didn't have to endure the same stomach-flipping fall as last night. I jumped from ledge to ledge until I'd reached the very corner of the building where a thick drainage pipe was fixed. It ran all the way down to the ground. I hurled myself at the pipe and slid down until my feet hit the grass.

I had been expecting us to make our way back into the building through another open window. Instead, my legs launched me into a full sprint through the vineyards. When woods came into view, it dawned on me where we were headed. Arron's residence. Building H looked nothing more than a small wooden cabin. Why Arron preferred to live in this tiny place as opposed to the comfortable apartments in the main building baffled me.

I withdrew from my pocket the key that we had found in my father's office the night before. It fit the lock perfectly. I swung the door open and stepped inside. The cabin consisted of a single room. There was no bed. No kitchen facilities. Not even a toilet. Just one large room that was mostly bare save for the wooden desk in the corner and an array of cabinets. I flung myself toward the cupboards and, as I had done in Aiden's office, began sifting through them.

The map must be in here, muttered the Elder.

Minutes passed by but we had still spotted no map. Just as I was starting to lose confidence that we would ever find this elusive piece of paper, my hands brushed over a small metal box at the back of one of the cupboards. My eyes scanned the room and settled on a cluster of paperclips on Arron's desk. I immediately bent one out of shape, stuck the end into the box's key hole and set to work trying to pick it.

I started to fear what would happen if Arron returned. I imagined that he would be making his way back already, wondering why Aiden had never shown up at Room 59. This idea didn't seem to deter the Elder. My hands picked relentlessly at the lock until finally, with a click, the lid popped open.

Inside was an old map. At first it looked identical to the one we'd found in Aiden's office and I wondered whether this would once again be the wrong map. But as my eyes scanned the paper further, it was clear that this one was far more detailed. Indeed some locations marked here were missing completely from Aiden's one.

My eyes scanned every inch of the parchment. It was as if he wanted to commit the entire thing to my memory to access at a later time.

Then it happened.

My ears picked up snapping twigs and rustling leaves. Someone was scurrying toward us through the vineyards. Not having time to lock the box properly, I simply closed the lid and shoved it back into its place. I scrambled around trying to restore each of the papers to its original file.

Then I slipped back out through the front door and let the latch lock behind us. I dove for shelter into some bushes that lined the entrance to the woods. Peering through the leaves, I saw Arron now less than a quarter of a mile away from the hut. I feared that he might have picked up the sudden flash of my form zipping out of the cabin, or the sound of the latch closing.

It appeared that my worries were unfounded, however, for he

walked directly inside and slammed the door behind him.

After about fifteen minutes, when Arron had still not reemerged from his cabin, the Elder dared to move me forward out of the bushes and send me tearing back through the vineyards toward the main building.

My mouth split into a wide grin as I heard myself whisper:

"Now the real work begins."

Chapter 20: Sofia

I circled the main building for several minutes looking for an open window on the ground floor. On finding none, I walked round to the kitchens, grabbed a rock from the ground and smashed through a window.

Something within the Elder had given way and it was now willing to sacrifice caution for speed.

The kitchens were empty at this time of night. I headed away from them and stepped into a dark corridor. Then I turned right into a small washing room. I made a beeline for the back of the room, behind the sinks and dishwashing machines, where I uncovered a large wooden trapdoor. I slid my hands through the two metal handles and hoisted it open to see a dark staircase leading down to some kind of basement or underground storage facility.

I lost no time in lowering myself down, pulling the heavy door shut above me. The staircase was winding and narrowed sharply. It was also unlit and, had it not been for my supernatural vision, I was sure I would have fallen and broken a leg.

Finally, the stairs disappeared and I found myself standing in a small rectangular room. A hunter sat outside a steel door, his head tilted down to a book on his lap. Still unnoticed, I approached the man and grabbed hold of his throat. I clamped a hand over his mouth to stifle his shouts and snapped his neck. His body now limp, I grabbed his arm and pulled him over to a scanner fixed to the right side of the door. I placed his thumb against the glass and the steel door clicked open. I rushed inside, dragging the hunter in with me.

The door locked behind us. Leaving the hunter dead on the ground, I walked forward through a narrow tunnel lined with fluorescent lights. The tunnel soon disappeared and I stood at the entrance of a circular chamber with a towering ceiling. The floors were made of black marble and the walls had been painted white.

The room seemed bare on first glance. It was only when I looked more carefully at the floor that I noticed three holes drilled into the marble, positioned at even intervals around the circumference of the room. I approached the one nearest to me and peered over the edge.

What on earth…

I was looking down into what appeared to be an endless tunnel. Its walls were made of a swirling translucent substance which I couldn't fathom for the life of me; although it had a bluish tinge, it certainly wasn't water. And yet I was sure that it wasn't smoke either. But it was the sight beyond that truly made me question my sanity. I was looking down at what appeared to be the night sky, a sea of endless black scattered with stars.

Maybe there was something in that goat's blood.

As soon as I extended my head past the edge of that crater, a strong suction tried to pull me downward. I had to stagger back and spread my legs apart to avoid being sucked in.

Then, without warning, my mouth opened wider than I could have imagined it was physically capable of stretching. Just as it felt like my jaw was about to snap, I drew in a deep breath and then exhaled. A black whirling substance emanated from my mouth, directed straight into the tunnel. It resembled the crater's walls, save for its color. *Light, swirling, ethereal.*

The edges of the tunnel closest to us reacted to it and started hissing and, before I knew it, disintegrating completely. This disintegration then spread to other parts of the tunnel, round and round its walls until the bluish substance had vanished from sight completely. The suction stopped, allowing the Elder to relax my stance. And then, in the time it took me to blink, the hole had vanished. In its place was nothing but the same black marble that covered the rest of the floor.

My head felt frighteningly dizzy and a haze settled over my eyes, a haze I hadn't felt since the witch in the Cells had worked her magic on me. The pain in my joints and muscles intensified and now I felt a new sensation; my skin was starting to itch and sting.

We don't have much time left, the Elder hissed.

I stumbled my way across the room and stopped at the rim of the second crater. Once again, my jaw stretched open as I drew in another deep lungful of air. Just as my lungs were about to burst, I exhaled more black substance. The tunnel's walls evaporated and the floor formed over it as if the hole had never existed.

Then my legs folded beneath me. The Elder tried to force them to stand but they kept crumpling. So instead he made me crawl toward the third crater.

I knew I didn't possess the stamina to exhale a third time. Of course, that didn't stop the Elder from trying. But as my jaw began to extend, my ears picked up a sudden movement at the entrance of the chamber. Before the Elder could even look toward the direction of the noise, the sound of iron striking bone reverberated around the room.

A searing pain erupted at the back of my head.

Then merciful unconsciousness stole me away as all faded to black.

Chapter 21: Derek

It had been nearly three days of agony. Aiden had forced me to respect Sofia's arbitrary "five days of privacy" rule. He had at least allowed me to go to her door each night and lock her inside the room.

As I made my way along the corridor early that morning to unlock her door, I considered breaking my promise to Aiden. My nightmares had intensified threefold over the past few nights and I didn't think I could stand her absence any longer.

I unlocked the door to her apartment and stepped inside.

"Sofia?" I called tentatively.

I was struck by how draughty the place felt. I walked to her bedroom and saw the windows wide open.

"Sofia?"

No. Not again. Not again.

I ran through each of the rooms. They were all empty. Retracing my steps into the bedroom, I rushed to the window and looked out, fearing to see Sofia's body crumpled on the ground below. I thanked the heavens that I saw no such thing.

She can't have jumped from this height. What on earth would she have been thinking?

Then I recalled her mad escape from the hut in broad daylight, and realized that I had been an utter fool to not suspect that she could have climbed out of the window, despite its ridiculous height.

But where would she have wanted to go so urgently that she couldn't have waited until morning?

Although she showed no visible signs of being possessed, I could no longer deny this as a possibility.

I raced out the door. Skidding across corridors and whizzing down stairs—for I had no patience to wait for elevators—I soon arrived outside Vivienne's apartment.

"Vivienne!" I smashed my fists against the door. "Open up! Hurry!" Several moments passed and I heard no sound of her approaching. I gripped the handle. Strangely, the door had been left unlocked.

I expected to find my sister still in bed at this early hour. But her apartment was vacant. Everything seemed to be in its proper place and I didn't note any signs of a struggle.

Next, I tried Cameron. Then Claudia. Then Eli. Then Landis. All apartments had unlocked doors. All empty. I knew Shadow the mutt stayed with Eli, but even Shadow was nowhere to be found.

Gavin. They must all be having a meeting at Gavin's place. I was aware of how ludicrous this conclusion was even as I thought it. But my mind was numb with panic. I had lost too much in too short a time. I couldn't bear the thought that something could have happened to them.

I ran to the room Gavin had been given. Room 93. I knocked and shouted his name. I continued to yell until a bleary-eyed Gavin appeared at the door, naked save for a towel wrapped around his waist.

"What the hell, Novak?" He scowled, peering down at his wristwatch. "It's five in the morning."

I pushed past him with such force that he fell to the floor. I searched the bathroom, kitchen and sitting room, and then ran to his bedroom. A female with jet-black hair stirred on the bed. She lifted her head, revealing her face. Zinnia. She let out a yelp and pulled the bed sheets higher up to cover her body.

Somebody *has come for a meeting at Gavin's place.*

"Get out!" she yelled at me, blood rising in her cheeks. "Bloody hell, Gavin. Why did you let him in!"

"I didn't." Gavin steamed into the room.

"They're gone," I gasped. "Sofia. Vivienne. Claudia. Cameron. Eli. Landis. Even Shadow, for heaven's sake. All the vampires have vanished."

"What? When did you last see them?" Gavin asked.

"I've been so tied up working with Aiden, I haven't been out of his office much. But it's been certainly less than three days since I saw each of them."

"Well, what about Aiden?" Zinnia said.

"He's my next stop."

I rushed to Aiden's quarters. But when he came to the door in his pajamas, rubbing sleep from his eyes, I knew that we had lost them.

When I repeated the news to him, the first thing he did was say, "Arron. We need to find him." He pulled on a dressing robe and we ran directly to the Hawk's cabin at the bottom of the fields.

We didn't even need to knock on the door. All the curtains of the small building had been pulled open. As we peered through the windows, it was clear that it was empty.

Chapter 22: Sofia

Icy water splashed on my face. Strong hands shook my shoulders. The stone felt cold beneath me and I tasted blood in my mouth. My entire body felt like I'd just been dug up from the grave.

"You thought you could fool me." A coarse voice spoke.

Fingers gripped the sides of my face and forced my eyelids open. A pair of pale grey eyes came into view. And the outline of a man's face…

"You caught me off guard, I'll grant you that much." The man stood up and began to pace the room. "But I do wonder, really, what was your game plan? Even if you had managed to wipe out the third gate, do you really believe the witches wouldn't just create more gates on demand?"

My mouth opened painfully and a voice emerged that was a shadow of my own. "Your ignorance never fails me." I let out a cackle. "Or perhaps the Ageless favored us over you when she revealed that the power to create gates died almost a century ago with the last of the Ancients. The witches have grown too weak to conjure up that kind of magic. They have become drunk with complacency. They no longer work to keep their power like the Ancients did when they were still fighting to protect The Sanctuary."

The man knelt down and gripped my jaw. "Should that be the case, we know exactly how to banish you now."

"You may have stormed The Keep, but we still have two gates. Remember that we weren't as foolish as to have all our gates in one room!" My cackling echoed around the room.

A kick hit my gut and blood spilled afresh from my mouth.

"Get up," the voice said.

My arms and legs tried to gather themselves up but heavy chains weighed them down. I was far too weak to bear the load. Hands gripped my waist and hauled me to my feet. I leaned back against the wall. By now, my vision had become a little clearer, clear enough to see that it was a familiar face that stared back at me.

"Let's see how long you survive here once your pretty vessel has expired." Arron grinned. "It's a long way back to The Shade and even farther to The Underground. You might fade away before you can reconnect with your source. That would be a mighty shame now, wouldn't it?"

"Oh, don't worry about that," I interrupted with a smile. "You're foolish enough to be holding plenty of other vessels here quite suitable for my habitation."

"I wouldn't count on that if I were you," was all Arron said as he left the dungeon, slamming the door behind him.

Chapter 23: Derek

Aiden told me to stay put while he went back to the main building in search of Arron. I waited outside the Hawk's cabin until noon, but after that I simply couldn't sit still any longer. The sun beat down on the grounds and bees buzzed around my head as I made my way back to the main building.

I wondered if Arron could have taken all the vampires to Aviary for some sort of experimentation, as he had done to Anna, Kyle and Ian. That he hadn't at least warned us of this when we were supposed to be cooperating grated at my nerves.

I passed the reception and ran up to Aiden's office. I knocked until the door swung open. Standing there in the doorway was Arron.

"Where were you? I've been waiting down at your cabin for hours…"

"Come in, Novak."

Aiden sat at the table, his head in his hands. He didn't look up.

Why didn't he bother to let me know he'd already found Arron?

"Aiden," I said, "what's going on?" He didn't reply. I turned to Arron who'd just reseated himself at the table and glared at him. "Where have all the vampires gone?"

"We don't know." His cool eyes settled on me.

"Don't talk to me like I'm stupid, Hawk. If you don't have anything to do with this, where would they have all gone suddenly?"

"How do you know that your wife isn't the one behind it? She's been acting strangely lately, hasn't she?"

Irritated by Aiden's continued silence, I walked up to him and shook him. "What's wrong with you?"

My father-in-law's face was ashen and he stared back at me blankly.

"Or," Arron continued, "they could all have gone for a walk in the woods during the night and lost their way. But what you're forgetting, Novak, is that none of this is my concern any more. I agreed to cooperate until we stormed the Keep and you were brought to Sofia. It's not my fault that you managed to lose her again. Do you even remember my two conditions for agreeing to help you storm the Keep?"

So much had happened since, and my mind was riddled with such confusion and panic, I could barely recall them now.

"No? Well then, let me remind you. Firstly, all the vampires we held in our custody were meant to be turned into humans. And secondly, Aiden agreed to become one of us and be transported to Aviary. You may recall that I allowed them to remain vampires on their plea that they weren't yet ready to become humans... a generous concession on my part, was it not? But now it's time for me to claim my second condition. I've waited long enough."

"No. No. Not now. You can't take him yet," I said, jumping to my feet. "Not before he's said goodbye to Sofia. She doesn't even know he made this deal with you."

I looked down at Aiden and shook him again, this time more violently. "Are you just accepting this? Where has your spirit gone? Where's the warrior I thought I knew?"

Finally he spoke, his voice cracking. "Derek, if I believed that I had even an ounce of control over this situation, I would fight. But we struck a deal with Arron."

And what about Rose? You would leave forever without even seeing her once? What about Ben? I would have said the words to Aiden, but I tried to avoid discussing my children in front of him whenever possible. I crouched down so that my eyes were level with his and begged, "Please, Aiden. Your daughter and I still need you."

"The house on the beachfront you told me about, the one you and Sofia visited. Do you remember that? I took the liberty of buying it for you. It's been transferred to both of your names. And all my wealth, properties and other assets I'm leaving to you." He reached into his pocket, pulling out a business card and a set of keys. "Mr. Campbell is the man you need to contact for further details. I've placed him in charge of my legal affairs. And here are the keys to the beach house." He put both items in my hands.

It was as if Aiden hadn't heard me.

"If I have no family to share it with," I said through gritted teeth, slamming my fist down on the table, "what use is any of this to me?"

"I think Aiden's made himself clear, Derek." Arron walked to Aiden's side and placed a hand on his shoulder.

"Don't touch him," I snapped. The heat in my palms rose to a dangerous level. But I had to control myself; I couldn't start a fire in Aiden's office. There were too many valuable documents here to risk destroying.

"Is that a threat?" Arron's brows arched and his grip on Aiden tightened.

Desperation coursed through my veins. I didn't have any semblance of a plan. All I knew was that Aiden simply couldn't leave with Arron. I walked over to the door and shut it, then stood myself in front of it, blocking their exit.

"Look, Derek," Arron said. "I don't want to fight with you." He walked over to me. "I'm sure we can settle this amicably." Before I realized what was happening, he'd withdrawn a syringe from his cloak and dug it deep into my neck. The effect was instant; although my consciousness remained, my limbs became paralyzed and I could no longer hold my own weight. I sank to the ground. "Thanks for understanding, I knew you'd come round in the end," the Hawk said before dragging Aiden out of the room and slamming the door shut.

"No!" I screamed, praying that someone would hear me. "Gavin! Zinnia! Somebody stop him!"

When two hours had passed with my screaming out and still nobody coming to my aid, I knew that it was already too late to save Aiden. Arron would have made off with him by now.

Is there only so much pain a man can stand before he becomes irreparably broken?

If such a threshold existed, I was sure that I had crossed it. My wife, my son, my sister, my closest friends... I'd lost them all. And now that Aiden was gone, my last true ally with any power, I didn't know where to draw hope from in the darkness.

It had been days now since the witch had promised to call a meeting. I didn't know why I'd expected anything other than more grief from her kind. Maintaining even a sliver of hope now seemed laughable to me.

Just as hopelessness was about to consume me, footsteps raced along the corridor outside. Two loud knocks sounded at the door.

"Help!" I shouted.

Yuri and Liana burst into the room. Their clothes were ripped and they were covered with cuts and bruises. It seemed so surreal to me that I considered perhaps the drug flowing through my veins was causing me to hallucinate.

"Derek!" they gasped in unison. Yuri wrapped his arms around me and pulled my motionless body upright.

Then Liana grabbed my chin and pulled my head to face her. Her eyes wide, she said, "Sofia is possessed by an Elder."

Chapter 24: Derek

"She's somewhere here at Headquarters," Yuri panted. "Her Elder brought her here to wreck the Guardians' gates. The only reason you didn't recognize her as being possessed is that one of their witches in The Shade figured out a way to disguise it."

Of course. Of course!

"And now she's disappeared again!" I said. "Sofia along with the other vampires from The Shade—Eli, Landis, Vivienne, Cameron, Claudia… The last time I saw them face to face was two or three days ago."

Liana's and Yuri's eyes lit up at the mention of their loved ones' names. Then Liana asked, "Who did this to you, Derek?"

"Arron. I tried to stop him but he… he took Aiden to Aviary." I let out a heavy sigh. "And I'd bet my life on it that he's responsible for the others' disappearances too."

"First things first." Yuri stood up and looked around the room. "We need to find you an antidote. You're of no use to anyone like this... Aha." He picked up the syringe Arron had stabbed me with from the floor and sniffed it. "We need to pay a visit to the emergency room."

"I wouldn't do that if I were you." Gavin had also entered the room, surveying the situation. "Yuri and Liana, you shouldn't be seen," Gavin said. "If the vampires were removed deliberately from this place, you two are also in danger. Zinnia's doing some investigation of her own about their disappearance, but until she reports back, you'd best keep out of sight as much as possible. You should both come to my room, and I'll help Derek get..."

"Wait a minute," I said. We'd been rushing ahead of ourselves so much that I hadn't even stopped to consider the obvious. "How on earth did you escape from The Shade? And how did you travel here, or even gain entrance into Headquarters?" I looked out of the window. "It's broad daylight!"

"The Elders were giving our bodies a rest," Liana said. "They'd left us in one of the caves alone. A witch... she just appeared out of nowhere. She said she was going to bring us here to you. Next thing we knew, we were standing outside this office. I don't know if she also helped out any other vampires or humans, but..."

"The Ageless," I muttered. "Where did she go?"

"I have no idea," said Yuri. "I asked if she would stay to help us, but she ignored my question and vanished."

"We have no time to waste, Derek. If the Elder hasn't been giving her enough breaks, I dread to think what state Sofia could be in now. The Ageless clearly isn't going to offer any more assistance," Liana urged. "I don't know what has happened to the others, but the witch did tell us where to find Sofia. She said that Arron has locked her in a dungeon located directly beneath the Atrium. The trapdoor leading to her cell is hidden within the armory."

Arron... I knew it. If Sofia was still possessed, I had no idea what I'd do even if I managed to reach her. All I knew was that I had to.

"Gavin," Yuri said, handing him the syringe, "run up to the emergency rooms and ask the nurse to give you an antidote to this paralyzer solution. If the nurse asks why you need it, just lie."

Once Gavin had left the room, I said to my two friends, "Gavin's right. You mustn't be seen by anyone. As soon as Gavin returns, you must go with him to his apartment and lock yourselves inside. Don't come out under any circumstances."

"But Derek!" Liana exclaimed. "You need our..."

"No, Liana. Neither of you will be useful for anything if you get caught and taken God knows where." I shuddered, thinking of Vivienne and the others.

Gavin returned five minutes later with a new syringe full of transparent liquid. He lost no time in stabbing the needle into the vein in my left wrist. Within several minutes, I had regained full control over my limbs. I stood up and looked around the room. "Now that Aiden is gone, we must be careful. A hundred times more careful," I warned. "As long as we stay in this place, we're completely at the mercy of Arron."

I nodded at Liana and Yuri and they begrudgingly headed toward the door. "Gavin," I said, "take them to your rooms and keep them safe while I'm gone."

We all exited the room, heading off in different directions. The Atrium was only five minutes away from Aiden's office and it wasn't long before I'd found the armory and located a dusty wooden trapdoor behind a tall cupboard. As I heaved it open, the smell of damp and rot invaded my nostrils. The place was lit with dim light bulbs fixed at intervals along the walls of the winding staircase. I moved down the steps, pulling the door shut above me, making as little noise as possible.

The dungeon came into view and, in the corner, a familiar figure lay curled up on the ground.

"Sofia?" I whispered, approaching her cautiously. She didn't stir. She was so still I feared for a moment that she was no longer breathing. Chains had been attached to her hands and feet. The skin around them was red and raw. She must have been tugging against them for hours. I brushed her long matted hair away from her face. Dried blood covered her mouth and her eyes were closed. I reached to touch her skin and was appalled by how coarse and dry it now felt. A yellowish color was developing in patches.

"Sofia." I spoke louder and with more urgency.

I dared to shake her shoulders. She remained still. Just as I was about to leave her side to look around the room for keys to the chains, her eyes shot open, only these were not Sofia's eyes. A translucent film had developed over them. Her mouth hung loosely as though she had lost control over her facial muscles.

Her breaths started coming in rasps. "Derek!" she wheezed. "Please, darling. I need b-blood. I'm dying of thirst."

Is this Sofia addressing me? Or is it the Elder?

Whatever the case, Sofia's body was clearly fading away and if sustaining her also meant sustaining the evil within her, so be it.

I lowered my wrist and coaxed her to take a bite. Instead, with an unexpected motion she placed her arms around my neck and dragged my head down toward her. She bit into the flesh beneath my ear and began sucking. After several seconds I felt a stinging, weak at first but growing stronger and more painful. *The Elder wants to turn me.*

I jerked away from her, wincing as her fangs tore through my skin. She tried to grab hold of me again, but I stepped away.

"What are you doing, Derek? Can't you see that I need you, my love? I'm dying! All the times I fed you my own blood, and this is how you repay me?"

Although I knew Sofia would never speak such words, there was an undercurrent of truth to them that didn't fail to make me feel a pang of guilt.

Sofia continued to cry out to me. "If you won't feed me, then please, melt away these chains. Free me, Derek! What are you waiting for?"

Although I still had no idea how to get Sofia out of this nightmare, doing the opposite of what the Elder was insisting upon was a good place to start.

"Stop playing games by hiding behind my wife. I know what you are." My voice boomed through the dungeon. "You saw what I did to one of your fellow Elders back at The Shade, didn't you? Leave my wife now, lest the same fate befall you."

Sofia's eyes rolled and she began to laugh. "As if you would risk your precious lover's life! Remember that your Corrine is not here to save the day this time. She's powerless now, as weak as a bee out of sting. We made sure of that after what she did. If you kill me, you kill Sofia."

"I don't need any witch." I spoke with confidence I didn't possess. "I inherited more powers than you can possibly imagine from Corrine's ancestor, Cora. I could have done it without her. And I will do it without her in a few moments if you don't comply. My patience is running thin."

So desperate was the situation, bluffing was the only tactic I could think of. I knew better than anyone that I couldn't unleash fire on Sofia's body without running the risk of killing her. I widened my stance as if gearing myself up for a fight and allowed a small flare to escape from my palms.

"I'm warning you. I'll count to three. One… Two…"

Before I could finish counting, a door unlatching echoed around the room. I whirled around to look up at the trapdoor, but from a different direction a deep voice I knew too well spoke.

"Oh, interesting. Very interesting."

Arron emerged from a steel door in a far corner of the dungeon. My first instinct was to stand protectively in front of Sofia.

"So," Arron said. "I'd actually come to put the girl out of her misery now, rather than make her suffer until the bitter end. But perhaps you'd like to do the honors yourself?"

He drew out a wooden stake from under his cloak and offered it to me. I knew too much about the Hawk to appeal to his better nature, for he had none. Just like all the other supernaturals we now found ourselves embroiled with.

Without hesitation, I shot fire at him. Black wings sprouted from his back and flew him out of the way, but he only narrowly dodged being burned.

"Don't touch her," I snarled.

"Derek, you must understand that your wife is long gone. She's nothing but an empty shell. Can't you see the symptoms of expiration? Even if you managed to expel the Elder, it's far too late. She'll never recover. Give her up."

He's lying. Sofia is still there. If I believed the Hawk's words I would start acting rashly and lose control over the powers I desperately needed to harness.

"Protect me, Derek!" Sofia's voice squealed from behind me.

"You lie!" I shouted at Arron, lunging forward. He was now hovering above me, his head nearly touching the ceiling, and I managed to jump and grab hold of one of his feet, pulling him to the ground. I dealt a blow to his face that sent him skidding across the room.

He got to his feet and red fury sparked in his darkened eyes. I had never seen Arron in his full Hawk form before. Now he transformed in front of me. His mouth and nose became a black beak with a razor-sharp edge, and talons grew out from where his human feet had been.

"You've made a terrible mistake, Derek"—he flew at me and pinned me against the wall, his hands tightening around my throat and his feet forcing my palms away from him—"to cross a Guardian the way you have."

He tilted his head back, preparing to dig the point of his beak right into my neck. Then he froze.

The steel door through which Arron had entered the room had just slammed shut.

Arron released me and we both looked frantically around the room. Open chains lay on the ground where Sofia had been. Next to them rested a cluster of keys. It must have fallen from Arron's pocket when I'd hurled him against the floor.

"No!" Arron hissed.

He spread his wings and flew toward the door, pulling it open. I raced after him. Just as I had reached the door, he tried to slam it in my face, but I forced it open with all my strength. We'd entered a tunnel which was far too small to hold his outstretched wings, so he rushed ahead on foot like me. I was mere inches behind him. Sofia staggered up ahead, but she disappeared from sight.

She had reached the end of the passageway. Arron and I emerged a few moments after her. We'd entered a circular chamber with high ceilings and a shiny black floor. I charged forward, desperate to reach Sofia before Arron could.

She was now kneeling in the corner of the room leaning over what appeared to be a dark hole in the floor. She inhaled deeply. Panic overtook me. I believed she was taking in her last breath.

Everything that happened next was a blur.

Arron elbowed me in the stomach and reached her before me. He caught hold of her waist and dragged her back, away from the hole. He pinned her down against the marble floor, both legs either side of her, and began to strike her with his fists. One more blow and I was sure that would have been the end of my already dying Sofia.

I grabbed the Hawk from behind and hauled him off of her. We both crashed to the floor.

"Burn off his wings!" Sofia panted. "Kill him, Derek! Save me!"

I couldn't afford to let Arron take flight again. I crawled onto his back, forcing his face against the floor. Grabbing hold of both wings, I let the heat rage up in my palms again. On feeling the rising heat, Arron began writhing beneath me more violently than ever.

"Wait!" he gasped out. I glanced up to see that Sofia had crawled her way back over to the hole in the floor. Her chest heaved in another strange inhalation.

"That is the last open gate to Aviary. Know that if the Elder destroys it, you will never be reunited with your son."

What?

That split second of distraction became my downfall. Arron took advantage of my shock to squirm away from me. This time, the Hawk lost no time in grabbing Sofia and lifting her up into the air. He moved so quickly that I couldn't latch onto him before he flew out of my reach.

"No!" I bellowed.

Arron grinned down at me from the lofty ceiling and laughed. "Watch as I rip her apart. You might even be able to catch some of her falling limbs. If you'd only cooperated, I would have made it quick. A stab through the heart was all I had intended, but you just had to go and make it so much worse for her…"

Sofia flailed in his grasp, her claws extended and trying to lash out at him. But she had no chance. He was a bird of prey and Sofia a snake in his talons.

I considered directing more fire toward him, but he deliberately held Sofia in such a position that the flames would completely engulf her before they even reached him.

"Derek! Help me!" Sofia screamed again. Arron had started running his sharp beak along the length of her shoulder blades, making his first mark on her. Etching out his first cut. Terror filled me as a few drops of her blood splashed onto the floor just a couple of feet away from where I stood.

Is this where our journey ends, Sofia?

After all that we survived together, all that we fought for?

Like this?

"Return the girl to the ground."

A silky voice boomed through the room and echoed off the walls. Even Arron looked bewildered.

The witch with long silvery hair stood at the entrance of the chamber. The witch I had already sworn would never be welcome in my life.

Arron's expression was of shock, but it turned to fury. "You dare give me orders, witch?"

"You heard me, Hawk. Bring her to me."

"Has a fit of madness overcome you? Since when did a Hawk obey a witch's command?"

The witch kept her steely glare on Arron.

"Since today. Return her to the ground. Or I will wipe out the final gate to Aviary myself."

A deathly silence fell over the chamber. Both Arron and Sofia's faces exuded the same astonishment. It was as though neither Arron or the Elder had ever seen a witch take a stand in this way.

The witches are giving up their neutral ground. There will be no going back for them now. This means outright war between all the realms.

The Ageless moved closer to the hole as if to signal that this was no bluff. Arron's face contorted with rage, but he did as the witch asked. He soared back down and dropped Sofia to the floor.

The moment Sofia landed with a thud, she scrambled up on all fours and started crawling feverishly toward the gate. This time it was me who grabbed her before she could reach her destination. She howled, trying to maim me with her claws and dig her teeth into my skin, but I held on tight. I gazed up at the witch with desperate eyes.

The witch nodded, as if she'd read my mind. She held out her palms. A strong gust of wind rushed past my body and settled over Sofia beneath me.

"No! No, Derek! Don't let her do this to me! Take me away from this place!" Sofia's eyes were lit with anguish and I knew then that the Elder realized what was coming. She turned her face toward the Ageless. Her eyeballs turned black as night and her voice transformed into a hiss. "Exorcise this vessel, witch, and Cruor will not spare you. We will never stop until we have infected your entire realm and inhabited each and every one of your bodies like carnivorous worms—"

"You can loosen your grip on her," the witch said, maintaining eye contact with me and ignoring the Elder's horrifying threats. "I now have control over her limbs."

I let go of Sofia and stood up, praying that the witch knew what she was doing. I willed all the heat I possessed in my body to well up beneath my fingertips. Sofia hissed and squirmed on the floor, still refusing giving up the fight. As soon as the witch began muttering beneath her breath, I knew that it was time.

I unleashed the fire all at once. It wrapped itself around Sofia's body, engulfing her in a tornado of flames. Her screams could be heard for several minutes. Those minutes were the most torturous of my life—not knowing how many of those screams were Sofia's.

Eventually she fell silent. Her body became motionless and the Ageless nodded at me, indicating that it was safe to relinquish the flames.

Beneath the billows of dark smoke lay Sofia's worn body. She looked so fragile I was afraid that just picking her up would cause her to fall to pieces. I immediately ran to her side, showered her face with frantic kisses, and eased her into my arms.

Emergency room. I have to get to the emergency room.

I needed to see her eyes open again soon, or I wasn't sure my heart could take it anymore. *What if Arron spoke the truth that Sofia's body is spent now?* I placed my ear against her chest. *Thank God there is a small heartbeat, however faint.*

"You can ruin this gate, witch." Arron's eyes glinted dangerously in the dim lighting. "Just remember that Aviary doesn't forget. And Aviary doesn't forgive."

Then without another word, he dove through the hole in the floor. After he'd vanished from sight, the Ageless stared down at the gate and began muttering to herself.

Ruin the gate... but... my son...

"Wait!" I shouted. "Arron said that my son is in Aviary."

"He had every reason to lie to you about that," she snapped.

"I know. But it's the only straw I have to cling to. We've hit dead end after dead end trying to locate my son. Even if there's one millionth of a chance that Arron could have spoken truth, it's the only lead I have." Balancing Sofia over my shoulder with one hand, I grabbed the witch's arm with the other and pulled her back from the edge of the gate.

"This is against the agreement I discussed with my council. They would never approve of this. Keeping this gate jeopardizes our entire strategy. I can't, Derek. I'm sorry."

"Please." My eyes blazed into hers. "Please."

From the Ageless' impatient expression, I was sure that she was about to destroy the gate. But then her eyes softened.

"Go now, then," she said. "You have four hours. I'll eliminate the gate on the strike of the hour whether you have returned or not."

"But I can't leave Sofia in this state. Please, just give me a few days..."

"Out of the question! I've just offered you four hours. Take it or leave it."

The choice was clear: act on the slight chance that I'd be able to locate my son in four hours, or tend to my wife. Leaving Sofia at this critical hour might mean leaving her forever. Even if I managed to return unscathed through the gate, Sofia might have passed away by then without me at her side.

"I can't leave Sofia now," I repeated, my shoulders sagging.

The witch returned to the edge of the gate.

Not wanting to witness the only possible clue to my son's whereabouts fade away, I left the chamber and ran back through the tunnel.

I'd been so focused on my son that I'd only just considered that Aiden too was supposed to be in Aviary now. *Sofia never even got to bid farewell. And what if Vivienne and the others have been taken there too?*

Silent tears ran down my cheeks as I gazed down at my wife's unconscious form.

CHAPTER 25: DEREK

As we emerged from the trapdoor, the bright lighting in the Atrium showed the state Sofia was in even more clearly. My arms were already wet with her blood from the wound Arron had inflicted on her, and her skin was so dry it had started to flake off. Yellow skin had formed around her eye sockets and her eyes were shut tightly. Bruises and scrapes covered every part of her body and blood dripped from the corners of her mouth—a mixture of hers and my own.

With Arron locked out, I felt safer taking Sofia directly to the emergency room to see one of the nurses. I insisted upon the same one who had helped Sofia when I first brought her to Headquarters after her escape from the hut.

The nurse's round face drained of all color when she saw Sofia.

"How in heavens…"

"Please," I gasped. "She's had an original vampire, an Elder, inhabit her body for far too long. Her heartbeat is weak. Please, hurry!"

I laid Sofia down on the nearest bed and looked up expectantly at the nurse.

"But… I have no idea what you're even talking about. What is an Elder? I have no experience with this!"

"She's an ordinary vampire now!" I said, looking around the room at shelves upon shelves of medication and equipment. "Immune blood. Try giving her some more immune blood. That's got to help…"

"But," the nurse stammered, "we have no more immune blood. It's all been used up."

"Check the cupboards again!" I yelled. "Or there must be some left in the lab from when they were carrying out their testing on Anna. Where is the lab?"

"It's too late for immune blood." A deep voice spoke from the entrance of the room.

"Ibrahim? What the hell are you doing here? How could you have left Rose and Corrine…"

"It's all right, Derek," Ibrahim said calmly. "My brother is there in my place. He's just as capable of protecting them as I am. I left them for Headquarters because the Ageless called on me to assist with The Sanctuary's orders."

"What orders?"

"Do you want me to stand here talking or do you want me to help your dying wife?" He approached Sofia's bed and looked down at her. "Only magic can help her body now… *maybe*. And I can't make any promises as to her mental condition even if we manage to heal her physically. A lot will depend on how much she fended off the darkness while the Elder was inhabiting her."

"So just… just… hurry up and do something!" I had my fingers against Sofia's pulse and could barely feel it anymore.

Ibrahim walked round the bed until he was standing above Sofia's head. He placed his hands either side of her face, then muttered a chant beneath his breath. He blew gently against Sofia's forehead. For ten excruciating minutes, nothing happened. No matter how much Ibrahim blew against Sofia, she remained unchanged, her pulse fading closer to nonexistent with every second that passed.

But then it happened. The spot where Ibrahim had been blowing on Sofia's forehead became smooth; all cracks and signs of bruises, bleeding and yellowing disappeared. Then this smoothness began to spread across the rest of Sofia's face, first down along her nose, then across her cheeks, around her mouth, down her chin and then further down her neck. Soon her arms smoothed out and her fingers and hands also gained fresh skin. The nurse ripped open her dress and we could see the healing travelling down her chest, to her stomach, then toward her legs, and finally her feet and toes.

I looked up at the warlock, who was watching intently. Despite the worry that was weighing me down, I couldn't help but marvel at his knowledge as a healer. I wondered if even Corrine could have worked that kind of magic on Sofia. Corrine normally needed potions to treat a patient.

But why is he helping Sofia? I wasn't naïve enough by now to think that the Ageless didn't have some kind of ulterior motive for wanting Sofia's body healed. But whatever the motive, it didn't matter now. All I could think about at that moment was getting Sofia to open her eyes again so I could lose myself in their beautiful green color.

And after several more minutes, I got my wish. Her eyes fluttered open, those stunning emerald-green irises I missed so much.

I knew as soon as she looked at me that she was back. My Sofia had returned to me.

"Derek," she whispered, reaching up and placing her hand on my cheek. Although it was still cold, I could somehow feel the warmth of her soul transcending the coldness of her skin.

All the emotions that had been pent up in me for so long in the pain of her absence, set themselves free all at once.

Seeing that Sofia now appeared to be in a stable condition, Ibrahim and the nurse left us alone in the compartment. Wordlessly, I rolled the stained nightgown off of Sofia's shoulders and pulled it away from her body. I fetched a warm towel from the sink and wiped her down. Then I grabbed a blanket and helped her into a sitting position, rolling it securely around her. Placing one arm around her waist and the other beneath her thighs, I lifted her off the bed and sat down there myself, placing Sofia on my lap. I buried my head against her chest and closed my eyes, relishing the sweet sound of her now steadily beating heart, reassurance that her healing a few moments ago had not been some kind of hallucination. My Sofia was back.

This was the first time since the night she'd given birth that I'd held her in my arms. The real Sofia. The love of my life. The person without whom all would be for nothing. *My ever-burning light. My break of day.*

She clutched my hair between her fingers and brushed her soft lips against my forehead. Her kisses made their way down the arch of my nose and then to my jawline. A small smile spread across her face as she said, "It's okay, Derek. I'm back."

Lifting my hands to her face, I pulled her toward me and tasted her lips, slowly at first, but then with more heat and passion than ever before. To have her respond in kind, unhindered by the Elder, was an ecstasy I wanted to lose myself in forever.

Chapter 26: Sofia

"Sofia... you have no idea how much I've craved you... how hungry I've been... to have you back in my arms... the real you," he whispered inbetween lavishing me with kisses. "Please, don't leave me again."

He'd carried me out of the emergency room and brought me back to his bedroom where he laid me down on the double bed. Unraveling me from the blanket, he tucked me beneath his sheets.

"You didn't find the fake one so hot, huh?" I allowed myself a small grin as he tore off his shirt so fast that it might as well have been on fire.

He climbed into bed and lay next to me. Shivers ran through me as the warmth of his bare skin pressed against the coldness of mine.

I recalled all the times during my possession that I'd wanted to reach out my hand and touch him, reassure him, apologize for my behavior, for leaving him, for causing him pain and suffering. Now that I was free from my prison, I could barely contain myself. All these repressed emotions erupted at once as my form melded with his.

I relished every slow caress, each heavy breath against my skin, each brush of his heated body against mine. Every sensation was heightened now that I could return in kind all that my heart felt for him. I quivered, this time my own pleasure manifesting.

As we both reached our climax, his electric-blue eyes never left mine. They allowed me a vision into his soul: all the hurt he'd endured at my hands, and all the love, relief, desire and hunger that now filled him up on seeing me again. I saw it all in those beautiful irises of his.

As we rolled to our sides, finally allowing ourselves to catch a breath, part of me wanted to just stay in that room, wrapped safely in his warmth, and never face reality again.

But there were too many questions burning in my mind to ignore for much longer.

CHAPTER 27: DEREK

"Any news about our son?" Sofia broke the silence.

How do I answer that without shattering her heart into a thousand pieces?

I brushed my fingers slowly through her hair.

"The truth is, I still don't know," I said. "During the time that you were insisting that you stay in your room, I was working with Aiden…" My voice trailed off at the mention of her father. "Sofia, I don't know how to tell you this but… Aiden's been taken to Aviary."

She clutched both of my hands and squeezed hard, her eyes widening. "What…" she stuttered. "But he'll come back soon, right? Along with Kyle and Anna and Ian?"

I heaved a sigh. "When you were first taken to The Blood Keep all those months ago, we were desperate to bring you back. One of Arron's conditions for helping us storm The Keep was that he wanted Aiden in Aviary… permanently." Her breaths started coming faster and tears welled in her eyes. "Please understand, Sofia, that I tried to object. I knew that you would never approve of Aiden's decision. But he simply wouldn't hear of it. Bringing you back was his first priority. And then, shortly before I found you in the dungeon, Arron took him. I tried to stop Arron. But he paralyzed me and got away."

"No... No!" She sobbed against my chest. "What is Arron going to do with him?"

"I doubt very much that he will harm Aiden. He claimed that he wanted to turn Aiden into one of them. A Hawk."

I wanted to alleviate Sofia's grief by suggesting that if Aiden had now been transformed into a big strong Hawk, he might be able to find his way back to Sofia. But now that the gates to the Aviary had been wiped out, I knew this was impossible and I didn't want to give her any false hopes.

She cried for several hours, and I held her all the while, stroking her and trying to give her whatever comfort I could.

I attempted to reel in my own despair over the possibility of having lost my sister forever too. Sofia needed me to be her rock at this time, and I couldn't melt away and leave her stranded in her own waves of grief. *Vivienne, will I ever see you again?*

Sofia eventually quieted down and concluded, "So there's been no progress on our baby."

I took a few deep breaths, trying to steady my voice. "I guess you didn't catch what Arron said to me amidst all the chaos back in that chamber. When I had him on the floor and was about to burn off his wings, you were on the verge of evaporating the last gate. He claimed that our son is in Aviary. After you passed out, Arron returned through the gate and the witch insisted on wiping it out after him. So... so there's no way that we could check now even if we wanted to."

I explained about the four hours the witch had offered me and why I had rejected the opportunity.

"I understand, Derek. I could never blame you. I-I just pray that Arron was lying and that Ben is still within this realm." She shut her eyes and breathed deeply. "What about the others? Oh God, Derek. You still don't know what the Elder made me do to Vivienne, Cameron and Claudia…"

Sofia didn't manage to finish her sentence. We were interrupted by a sharp knock at the door.

"Stay here, I'll get it," I said, grabbing a spare sheet and wrapping it around my waist.

I looked through the peephole and saw Gavin and Zinnia. As soon as I opened the door, the flustered pair barged in.

"It's just Zinnia and Gavin," I called to Sofia, warning her to cover up so she wouldn't get the same shock I had given Zinnia earlier that morning.

"No, wait, keep the door open," Zinnia panted. "There's Craig too. He's slower and just fell a bit behind us."

I poked my head out of the door and sure enough, Craig was limping toward me on crutches. His right leg was wrapped in a thick cast.

"Whatever happened to *you*?" I asked.

"Just let me sit down first," he said, wincing.

I beckoned them all through to the sitting room before going into the bedroom to find something more suitable to cover myself with. Sofia was already pulling on a dressing gown. We both went next door and they all gasped on seeing Sofia.

"Well, at least you found Sofia, Derek," Gavin said. "We got news on the others, but not Sofia, so I was really starting to worry. Whatever happened to you, girl?"

"Her story can come later," I interrupted. "What news on the others?"

"Well," Zinnia began, "after we suspected Arron might have been involved in their disappearance, that kind of switched a lightbulb on in my head." I held my breath, fearing the worst. "I knew from experience that Arron nearly always uses Craig here to carry out his dirty jobs, the ones that aren't made common knowledge among the community of hunters. Ain't that right, Craig?"

Craig grimaced.

"So," Zinnia continued, "I went to his apartment and when he opened the door with his broken leg, it was kinda obvious something was up. I managed to figure out a way to manipulate him for information…"

"You make what you did sound skillful," Craig interrupted with a scowl. "Threatened an invalid was all she did. Put a knife to my goddamn throat."

"Well, anyway, Craig, come on," Zinnia said nonchalantly. "Tell them what happened to the vampires."

Craig cleared his throat and said, "Orders came from Arron to sneak into the vampires' rooms and paralyze them. Then he wanted us to transport them all to one of the boats and ship them off. He didn't want them at Headquarters any more."

At least they haven't been taken to Aviary. But this alternative didn't sound too appealing either.

"Ship them off where?" I asked.

"Now listen here." Craig's eyes narrowed on me. "If Arron ever finds out that I'm the one who told you…"

"You don't need to worry about that. Arron's gone. All the Guardians have left this place. The gates between this realm and Aviary are all destroyed. Now tell me, where did you ship them off to?"

"We just took them a few miles out to sea and dropped anchor. I honestly don't know what he was planning to do with them after that, or why he wanted them gone in the first place…. but damn, it was hard work gathering up that feisty one. Your sister, Vivienne." He let out a dry chuckle. "She ripped her claws right through my leg just as I was injecting her."

His mention of my sister sent an urge rushing through me to finish the job, but I couldn't injure him further. He had to be our guide.

"All right," I said. "Now that we have Sofia, the first thing we need to do is find the other vampires. *You,* Craig, are going to help us to the shore and navigate a boat for us. I'm sure Zinnia will happily volunteer to make sure you cooperate."

"Sure, Derek." She flashed a sideways grin at Craig and half withdrew a dagger strapped to her belt.

"Gavin, where are Yuri and Liana?" I asked.

"They're still at my place. They're fine, don't worry. I even found some animal blood for them," Gavin replied. Sofia relaxed a little beside me at his assurance.

"Go fetch them now. My room is nearest to the back exit of the building. We'll leave together."

Once Gavin had left, I began to think out loud. "I want all of us out of Headquarters. The Hawks may be gone, but we're still surrounded by people like Craig who hate vampires. Not all seem to have had such a drastic change of heart as Zinnia here. And now Aiden is gone too, it's just not safe for us any longer."

"But where, Derek? Where can we possibly go?" Sofia asked.

"Zinnia, take Craig into the bedroom," I said. "I don't want him to hear this discussion."

Craig jumped up to his feet before Zinnia could brandish her knife at him. He walked obediently into the next room.

I walked over to the sofa where I had dumped my jeans, reached into their pockets, and drew out the keys and the business card Arron had handed me before his departure.

"Remember that beach house we visited together in California? I'd mentioned it in passing to Aiden. I thought it odd he asked me for the exact address of the place, but I didn't expect him to just go ahead and buy it." I rattled the keys in front of her and she clasped a hand to her mouth. "Well, he did. And he's left it in our names along with the rest of his fortune. Aiden loved you more than you could ever imagine, Sofia."

She broke down into tears again as she took the keys from my hand and stared at them. "He sacrificed himself for me... for us... to have a future together."

I allowed her a few minutes before I had no choice but to interrupt. "We need to get a move on, my love." She wiped the tears from her eyes and nodded. "Let's get dressed properly and then once Gavin has returned with Liana and Yuri, we must leave this place immediately."

I found a fresh pair of jeans and a new shirt and pulled them on. Then I grabbed a small bag in which I placed the keys, the business card and my phone, and fastened it to my belt. Sofia looked around the room with a bewildered expression on her face. I realized we had nothing that she could wear. None of my clothes fit her, and I didn't want to waste time having Zinnia return to her chambers for some spare clothes, so she had to make do with her dressing gown.

There was another knock at the door. On seeing our two vampire friends enter the room with Gavin, Sofia leapt into their arms, kissing their cheeks and embracing them.

"Thank heavens you got out," she said.

Once I'd called Craig and Zinnia back, we were ready to head off. We made our way down to the kitchens, which were empty at this late hour. We exited through the back door and walked toward a collection of motor buggies near the entrance of the main building. We all bundled into two of them, Zinnia driving one and Gavin driving the other. Zinnia made sure to keep Craig sandwiched between Yuri and Liana. We drove until we reached the main electronic gates, where two guards were waiting to inspect us.

"We're on orders from Arron to transport these vampires out to sea along with the others," Zinnia said. "Ain't that right, Craig?"

Craig grunted, but this seemed to pacify the guards, for they let us go.

We sped through the gates and hit the winding dirt road. After about forty minutes of driving, I began to catch the scent of salt in the air. We drove onto a sandy beach, where we parked, got out of the vehicles and made our way toward the silhouette of several boats stationed in a small private harbor.

There, we were met with another hunter whose job it clearly was to guard the vessels. When the man asked for explanation for our visit, Zinnia didn't say a word. She pulled out a little gun from her pocket and shot a dart into his neck.

"Just a tranquilizer," she muttered when he collapsed to the floor unconscious. "He'll be all right by the morning." She leaned over and grabbed a set of keys from behind his desk.

As we walked over to a speedboat, Sofia asked the question that had been nagging at the back of my mind ever since I'd reunited with Zinnia.

"Why are you doing this, Zinnia? I thought you hated us."

Zinnia paused. "It's a good question. It's one I've asked of myself many, many times recently. Maybe it's got something to do with hanging around with this guy." She flicked a finger in the direction of Gavin, who was walking alongside her. "He seems to like and respect you two. So maybe it rubbed off on me a bit. Or maybe, just maybe, it runs a little deeper than that."

Gavin looked mortally offended. "And there I was thinking that you were just blinded by my shocking good looks."

Zinnia jabbed him in the ribs. "Despite what you might think, Sofia, I've always been one to follow rather than lead. I like to have a strong leader I can place my faith in. Aiden was that for me, until his visit to The Shade… and then he changed. It unsettled me at first, but after a while I realized that he was right. You know what he told me? He said, 'Revenge is not a cause, it's a controlling obsession'. The more I thought about it, the more I realized I wanted to distance myself from the hunters' cause, which of course we now know was only ever the Guardians' cause." She opened up the door to the speedboat and let us all in. "And, as I said, I like having a leader. I have a feeling in my bones for what makes a good one. I've come to like and respect you both, Derek and Sofia. I saw what you managed to accomplish at The Shade and I believe in what you're fighting for. My bones approve of you."

With that, she inserted the key into the ignition and started up the engine.

"Craig!" Zinnia sounded like a nagging housewife as she called him over. "Come here and navigate this thing." Craig shuffled over and took hold of the controls. "And if you want to return to shore with your balls still attached, don't even think about getting us lost."

I took a seat next to Sofia on the long bench as the boat lurched forward. I worried that Craig would get lost unintentionally, since it was so dark, and the strong gusts of wind that had just started up didn't make our path through the waves any easier.

"Did you leave any hunters on the ship with them?" I asked Craig nervously.

"Yep, at least half a dozen. And they'll be armed, of course," he said. "I'd like to see how you manage to talk yourself out of that one, missy," he added to Zinnia.

The others seated on the bench looked as concerned as I felt. *Damn. How could I not have considered that possibility before we set off?* It seemed blindingly obvious to me now that Arron wouldn't have left the ship unguarded.

"Zinnia and I did consider that possibility, actually." Gavin whisked out four handguns from beneath his overcoat.

"And if I'm not mistaken," Zinnia said, "they normally keep at least a few backup weapons on these boats." She opened a small wooden cupboard beneath one of the benches. "Aha. There are two more guns here. And plenty of bullets too."

"Good," I said. "Sofia should stay on the boat with Craig. Remember, Craig, she's got claws too now, along with a nice sharp set of fangs, and she's more than ready to use them, believe me." I pointed to the bite marks on my arms and neck. "So don't even think about trying anything with her. Make sure we bring all arms with us onto the boat so there's nothing here Craig could possibly find and use against her."

"Wait, hold on, guys," Sofia said. "Zinnia, why can't you just get Craig to tell them that Arron sent orders to have them brought back to shore? It's not like they can call Arron up and check."

"These hunters are part of Arron's inner circle," Zinnia explained. "And I learned from Craig that any drastic change of course during a mission requires direct approval from Arron. So even our darling Craig's word may not be enough. And if they find that they can't contact Arron, that could arouse suspicion."

"We'll try to avoid a fight at all costs. I assure you that much," I said to Sofia, brushing a hand over her knee. Then we set to work gathering up weapons and hiding them beneath our clothing.

"As soon as we board the ship, we locate the vampires," I said. "Yuri and Liana, you're in charge of detecting their scent and leading the way toward them. Gavin, Zinnia and myself will watch everyone's backs."

"I'm really hoping most of them will be asleep at this hour," Gavin muttered. "Getting into a fight with hunters is going to be way too messy. I'm sure they have those UV guns on board..."

I gulped as I remembered the effect those guns had on vampires. Indeed, my own brother had died from one of their bullets.

After several more tense minutes had passed, Craig called out, "All right, people. Look to your right. That's the ship."

We all gazed in the direction his finger was pointing in. A large black ship bobbed on the waves. No lights shone through any of the windows. A hopeful first sign.

I lowered my voice and said, "Craig, switch off the boat's lights immediately and navigate us as near to the vessel as possible without bumping into it. And stay close to it until we return. Now, everyone except Sofia follow me up to the roof."

We took it in turns to lean out of the window and pull ourselves onto the metal rack above, now fully exposed to the powerful wind and cold spray.

"Hold on tight, guys. We can't afford to have anyone falling overboard," Zinnia warned.

Craig did as I had instructed and a few moments later, we were close enough to the ship to risk the leap. I fixed my eyes on the rail lining the deck and jumped. My hands hit the iron and I managed to grab hold of it. I pulled myself over the barrier and my feet landed on the wooden floor. My comrades were waiting on the roof of the speedboat.

"Be careful," I hissed. "It's slippery. One at a time."

Zinnia jumped next. I grabbed hold of her wrists the minute she hit the side of the ship and lifted her over. Next came Liana. Then Yuri. And finally, Gavin.

Once our feet were all planted firmly onboard, Zinnia led the way to a trapdoor and we descended a set of steps. "Good," she whispered. "I know this ship. I've been on it before."

Liana waved at us for attention.

"Vampires," she mouthed, sniffing the air. Yuri looked at her and nodded in agreement. She pointed to the ground.

"Okay, the lowest floor," Zinnia said. We descended another narrow flight of stairs and found ourselves in a long unlit room whose walls were lined with small cells.

"Claudia!" Yuri darted to the first cell on our right. A few seconds later, Liana had rushed to the third cell along, spotting Cameron. And then it was my turn; I saw my beloved sister. She'd been huddled in the corner but on seeing me, she rushed to the bars and her face lit up.

"Derek!" she choked. "I thought you might never find us."

"We're going to get you out of here." I reached for her hands through the bars and squeezed them tight. "Zinnia!" I called. "Have you found the keys?"

"Not yet," she said from across the room. She'd been foraging through the drawers of a desk in the far end of the room.

"The keys are up there!" Vivienne said, pointing to a hook in the ceiling from which hung a dozen keys. "One of the hunters hung them right in front of us, just out of reach. A nice form of torture."

I jumped and unhooked the keys. I started fumbling with each one until the lock to Vivienne's cell finally clicked and the door swung open.

She flung herself into my arms. We hugged briefly, but then I pulled away to move on to the next cell. Eli had been put next door to Vivienne. He looked up at me with weary eyes, but his face broke out into a smile.

"Good job, Derek. We were really starting to worry," Eli said.

Once I'd freed Eli, he rushed out to greet his brother Yuri. I quickly moved on to the others: Cameron, Landis and Claudia.

Just as we'd gathered everyone together, a snarl emerged from the far corner of the prison. The snarl grew into a bark. *Oh, no. No.* I'd forgotten about the dog in my frenzy and we were about to leave without him. He continued to bark and jump against the bars.

"Shut that dog up!" Zinnia seethed. "He's going to get us all caught!"

I bolted over to his cell and unlocked it. He immediately jumped up at me and began licking my face. I grabbed his collar and led him to Eli, who bent down and tried to calm the huge animal.

But it was too late. Footsteps sounded over our heads. Gavin, who had been keeping watch on the floor above, came rushing down the staircase.

"Listen to me! All vampires, get back into your cells! Yuri and Liana, find cells of your own and shut the doors behind you! Just do as I say!"

Although they all looked bewildered, they obeyed. I took Shadow from Eli and shoved him back into his cell too, pushing the door until the lock clicked. Quickly catching on to Gavin's train of thought, I swung the keys back over the hook on the ceiling.

Everyone returned to their places just in time before two burly young hunters came staggering down the steps.

Zinnia moved forward and greeted them. "Oh, hey, Joshua. Hey, Tyler," she said smoothly. "How are you two? We just came to add a couple more vampires to the lot. Arron's orders, ya know. Sorry we disturbed you. I didn't realize you had a noisy dog down here too. He got a bit over-excited."

She walked over and wrapped an arm around both men's shoulders, kissing them each on the cheek.

"It's been a while since I've seen you two. I've missed you."

The clenching of Gavin's jaw didn't escape my notice. But otherwise, he was doing a good job at keeping his face expressionless.

"I missed you too, Zinnia," Joshua said, returning the kiss. From the slur of his voice and the redness of both men's eyes, the two had poured themselves a glass of wine too many.

Tyler looked a little more suspicious as he glanced around the room. "Who are those two? And what are they doing here?" He narrowed his eyes on Gavin and me, who were the only others outside of the cells.

"Oh, don't mind them," Zinnia purred. "They're new recruits at Headquarters and helped me bring the vamps here." She snaked her arm around Tyler's waist and stood on her tiptoes so her face was barely an inch away from his. "Mmm. I'm pretty thirsty actually. I fancy some of what you two have been having. Smells good. And, God knows, it's been ages since I've spent a night in good company."

Tyler glanced around the room once more but seemed too wound up in Zinnia's charms to give the situation much further thought. The three of them made their way back up toward the exit.

Just as Zinnia was about to close the door behind them, she threw a quick glance back at Gavin and mouthed, "I'm sorry."

Once their footsteps had faded away, Gavin scowled, but he

shrugged it off quickly. "Well, she did what she had to do," he said. "Now, before anything else happens, let's get these vampires out of here."

I reopened all the locks, which was thankfully easier the second time around. Eli grabbed hold of Shadow once again and we all climbed up the steps and hurried across the top deck, back to the metal railing.

The speedboat was still where we had left it. Gavin leaped onto the roof first, and then I assisted each vampire one by one in jumping over, where Gavin waited to help them keep their balance and lower them down through the window.

Finally, only Shadow and myself were left on the ship. I helped the massive animal perch on the edge of the railing and hurled him off. He landed with a thud on the roof and very nearly sent Gavin skidding into the rough waters. Eli reached out from below and helped Shadow climb clumsily down into the boat's control room, almost falling into the waves himself.

I looked back across the dark wet deck toward the direction in which Zinnia had vanished. I wondered what the men would do to her in the morning once they'd realized all the vampires had vanished during the night.

Something told me though that the small hunter would find a way to wrangle herself out of it. I chuckled softly before thrusting myself off the railing.

CHAPTER 28: SOFIA

Craig had been surprisingly easy to deal with. He'd made no attempt to give me trouble as we waited for Derek and the others to return. He barely spoke a word. Admittedly, I'd had my claws extended the entire time we were sitting together, and had placed my hands on my knees so they were clearly visible to him.

As soon as they had arrived back and slid safely down into the boat's cockpit, Derek barked at Craig to start the engine and speed us away.

Despite the cabin now being cramped—with a soggy Shadow hogging an unholy amount of space—Derek squeezed over to me. I reached for his wet face and examined him, relieved that he appeared to be unscathed. He slid his hands down my body and wrapped them around my hips, pulling me closer to him in a tight embrace. He caught my lips between his and kissed me intensely. He didn't say anything, but I knew from the look in his eyes what was going through his mind. He'd been afraid something could have gone wrong while I was alone with Craig.

Our kiss was interrupted rather unceremoniously by a third party. Something coarse and wet slapped against my cheek. Shadow was attacking me with his smelly snake-like tongue.

"Urgh, thanks." I grimaced, wiping my face against my sleeve. "It's good to see you again too, Shadow." The dog placed his front paws on my knees, flattening them against the hard wooden bench.

Derek grabbed the mutt's collar and yanked him back down to the ground on all fours, where Shadow continued to brandish his tongue, attempting to lavish me with more uninvited affection. Despite the surprise, I really had no right to feel irritated with Shadow. He'd saved my life and that of my two babies in carrying me out of the Keep, and endured great personal suffering in doing so.

"There, boy," I said, grabbing his enormous head between my hands and giving him a generous ear scratch. He settled down contentedly at my feet.

I looked around the cabin to get a better look at our newly arrived passengers. The first sight that met my eyes made me break out into a wide smile. Liana and Cameron sat opposite us. Cameron's body shook with tears of joy as he held Liana in his arms and showered her with kisses.

And next to them sat Claudia and Yuri. The feisty blonde had placed herself on Yuri's lap, her small legs wrapped around his waist. They kissed as though they were having a competition of who could get to the back of the other's throat first. I diverted my gaze, feeling uncomfortable watching a scene that was escalating too rapidly to belong anywhere other than their bedroom. I caught Derek's eye and we both broke out giggling. When we noticed Eli sitting at an awkward angle nearby, positioned to distract himself from the couple, we laughed even harder.

Taking pity on him, Derek tugged on Shadow's collar. "Come on, boy. Stand up. Go to Daddy over there in the corner. He looks like he's in need of some company." Eli glanced over at us and smiled with embarrassment, mouthing a "thank you" to Derek when Shadow got up and made his way over to his master.

Then my eyes fell on Vivienne in the far corner and any joy I'd just felt vanished. Her eyes were fixed on the ground and beads of tears trickled silently down her cheeks. Landis sat next to her, an arm placed around her shoulder, although he too looked devastated.

Derek followed my gaze and, on noticing her too, he looked back at me. "My sister deserves more than this. She's sacrificed more than any of us."

"I-I don't think Xavier made it, Derek," I whispered, recalling the state of his body when the Elder had transferred to me. I hadn't seen him since and neither had Ashley. It seemed that Yuri and Liana had no news of the man either.

Derek held his head in his hands and fell silent, a silence that lasted until Craig addressed him.

"We're back at the port. What now?"

"We'll drop you off here," Derek said. "You're free to go back to Headquarters."

Craig looked suspiciously at Derek, but then he nodded and limped his way out of the boat. He scurried away from the port and drove off in one of the buggies still parked up on the beach.

I looked up at Derek in question, as did Gavin. "He's of no use to us any more. And I don't want him knowing the location of our new home." Then Derek said, "Liana, you're the most experienced captain on this boat. I need you to navigate us to the beach where our new house is."

Liana pulled herself away from Cameron's arms and stood up.

"Well, I'll do my best. I really hope there are some decent maps here." She began searching through a drawer beneath the controls and pulled out several large maps, spreading them out against the dashboard. Derek went over to her, gave her the address and helped her locate our villa. Once Liana seemed to be confident of our destination, she took Craig's place and the boat went shooting forward.

"We need to hurry," said Derek. "We've only a few more hours until the sun starts to rise."

By the time we arrived at the villa, daybreak looked about half an hour away. Liana steered the boat toward the shore until it hit shallow waters, at which point we all abandoned it. We jumped into the ocean and rushed across the sand, and then up the stairs to the boulevard our house was situated on.

A wave of nostalgia hit me as we arrived outside our charming home. I remembered all too clearly visiting the place months ago with Derek. I remembered how we'd fantasized about raising a family here. A dream that now seemed destined to be elusive.

Derek was the first to arrive at the front door. He reached for the keys from his pocket and unlocked it. We all bundled inside, leaving a trail of dirt behind us on the white floors. Shadow shook his giant mane, spraying the pale walls with mud.

My immediate concern was the impending sunshine. Thankfully, the house had come furnished and blinds lined the windows.

Once we'd closed the blinds, it was clear that everyone was itching for some rest, or in a certain couple's case, privacy. It had been a long, stressful night.

"Is there a basement here, Sofia?" Eli asked me politely, Shadow trailing along behind him.

"Um... let's take a look." We found the door to a large basement located in the washing room. We descended the steps and Eli looked around, nodding.

"This looks like a good place for Shadow to rest for now, out of everyone's way."

Shadow padded over to a corner and nestled down. Then I took Eli upstairs to find him a bedroom that hadn't already been snagged by the others. It turned out that he had to share with Landis. The two couples had already locked themselves up and Vivienne must have already retreated into a room by herself.

I wished Eli and Landis goodnight before heading off to find Derek. He wasn't in the master bedroom that had been left for us to share. I went down the stairs and into the living room, but only saw Gavin lying on the sofa.

Then voices came from the kitchen. Derek stood leaning against the kitchen counter, in conversation with a tall dark-haired man I immediately recognized as Ibrahim.

As soon as Derek saw me enter, he said, "Ibrahim, I hear what you're saying. But let's please discuss all this in a few hours once we've had some rest. The bedrooms are all taken but if you want to stay here, there's plenty of comfortable sofa space in the living room."

Ibrahim nodded and gave me a brief smile before leaving the room.

"How come he's here all of a sudden?" I asked.

"Sofia," Derek said sleepily, "let's talk about it in a few hours. We both need to get some rest." Without waiting for my response, he picked me up and whisked me to our bedroom.

We undressed and tucked ourselves under the freshly starched sheets. A suspicious noise was starting to emanate from the direction of Claudia and Yuri's room. I cuddled up next to Derek and muttered, "Well, this sure isn't the housewarming party I would have expected."

Chapter 29: Derek

I woke up after six hours of sleep. The temperature in the room had risen considerably. I moved the sheets away from my body and looked down to see Sofia still asleep, her head against my chest. I lifted her head gently onto the pillow and wriggled down in bed so my face was level with hers. I placed a hand against her back and pulled her closer, pressing my lips against her neck and breathing in her scent. She stirred after several minutes and looked up at me. Confusion spread across her face.

"That was strange. I thought for a second that I was back at your penthouse in The Shade," she said, rubbing her eyes. Then she squeezed my hand and looked at me seriously. "We need to rescue The Shade, Derek. Our people are in a terrible state, I can't even begin to describe…"

"That's partly what I was talking to Ibrahim about last night." I slid out of bed and began getting dressed. "Let's go down and continue that conversation with you present this time." She found a clean dressing gown in the bathroom cupboard and fastened it around her.

When we arrived downstairs, Ibrahim was already waiting for us in the kitchen. We both greeted him with a nod and took seats next to him at the table.

"So, as I was saying," Ibrahim said, "the council's next plan is to finish wiping out the gates to Cruor. I've just come directly from destroying the gate at The Underground. Now the only gate to Cruor that remains is the one within the witch's temple at The Shade."

"I'm curious," Sofia said. "Why do you witches even need our help in wiping out The Shade's gate when you seemed to be able to ruin The Underground's without much problem?"

"Because," Ibrahim replied, "the job at The Underground was easier. The vast majority of the Elders have gathered at The Shade because that's where most of the vessels and humans are."

"And how exactly do you propose that we destroy The Shade's gates when the place is swarming with Elders and vessels?" I asked.

"Firstly, none of the vampires here would accompany us. That would just provide them with more vessels. I would call on some more witches to help from The Sanctuary."

Gavin stepped into the room, followed by Zinnia.

Momentarily distracted from our discussion, I asked Zinnia, "How on earth did you get back?"

"Oh, it wasn't too difficult. I just shifted the blame to you two. Told them that you and Gavin must have run off with the vampires and that I had nothing to do with it. Tyler didn't seem to believe me, but I managed to get Joshua on my side, who convinced him to let me go. They dropped me back at the port where I called Gavin's number. I stole one of the boats and here I am."

Sofia placed a hand on my arm, resuming our conversation. "I understand why vampires are of no use to this mission, and the same for humans"—she looked pointedly at Zinnia and Gavin—"but the others aren't going to like this. They're going to want to fight for The Shade."

"In which case, to avoid wasting time arguing with them, we should leave now before they all wake up," Ibrahim said.

Sofia tensed up beside me and tightened her grip on my arm. "You didn't finish explaining the plan to Derek," she said. "How exactly are you going to go about this?"

"We'll have to play it by ear. We don't know what the exact situation will be before we arrive," Ibrahim said. "But we'll have help. And as with The Underground, we have the advantage of surprise on our side. As long as we're quick... I'm hoping the Elders at The Shade haven't yet received news that the witches ruined The Underground's gate." He snapped his fingers and a dozen witches and warlocks wearing dark grey robes entered the kitchen.

I hugged Sofia and looked deep into her eyes. "Keep everyone safe. Don't allow anyone to leave the house. But you'll need blood. Zinnia and Gavin will stay here and help you cope."

Then, before I could offer her words of comfort that I knew she desperately needed, Ibrahim's hand rested on my shoulder, and the next minute, I couldn't see anything at all. A blur of colors shrouded my eyes.

CHAPTER 30: DEREK

When my vision eventually returned, I was floating in the sea beneath a starry night's sky. Ibrahim swam beside me along with his army from The Sanctuary. It didn't take long to spot a familiar outline in the distance; we were about a quarter of a mile away from my lighthouse.

Ibrahim nodded and we swam to land, hoisting ourselves up on the rocks just below the tall building.

"The sooner we reach the temple, the better. Derek, try to remain hidden from view."

The witches gathered around me and I crouched down so that my head was not visible above them as we walked. We moved away from the rocky area, past the Port, and entered the woods, moving swiftly toward the Sanctuary. My whole body tensed when a symphony of screams pierced through the atmosphere.

"What was that?" I whispered to Ibrahim.

"You don't want to know."

It felt like we had been running through the woods for about half an hour, the screams unrelenting. Eventually we reached the spot where the trees ended and the clearing outside the temple began. We crouched down in some bushes and surveyed the situation.

Several tall figures were huddled around the fountain. One of them I recognized instantly: Ashley. The other faces were familiar but I couldn't put names to them—vampires whom, although they were citizens of The Shade, I had never personally spoken to. And then I spotted a vampire less than half the size of the others and I realized it was Abby.

The group stood in front of our destination, the temple. There was no way we could walk past them without being noticed.

I looked sideways at Ibrahim through the shrubbery. His brows furrowed, he appeared to be thinking furiously. This surprised me, because our next step seemed obvious to me.

"Just do your disappearing trick. Vanish us from here and manifest us again inside the temple," I whispered.

He shook his head and looked at me like I'd just come up with the most stupid idea in the world. "Just trust me, all right?"

Then, without any warning, he sprang out of the bushes. My first instinct was to grab him and pull him back, but two witches yanked me back down into a sitting position. I wasn't used to being kept in the dark and following orders blindly.

"Shhh. Just watch, Derek. And have faith in Ibrahim. We will tell you when to move and what to do when the time comes," an elderly-looking witch next to me said, patting my shoulder with her wizened hand.

As soon as the group of vampires caught sight of Ibrahim approaching, they froze and stared at him. At first, I feared the worst—the Elders had already got wind of the witches' gate-wiping rampage. But it appeared that they had not.

"Well, well, well. If it isn't the Ageless' cousin himself. What brings you here, warlock?" Ashley stepped forward. Although her eyes were clear like Sofia's had been, the strange yellowing of her skin was evidence enough that she too was being inhabited by an Elder.

"Yes, do tell. You'd better have a good excuse for disturbing us," Abby piped up.

Abby apparently hadn't had the same treatment as Ashley and Sofia. Her eyes were glazed over with a translucent film and her mouth split open in an awkward smile, her expression mismatched with her age.

"I'm here to meet with the Elder in charge." Ibrahim's voice remained steady and if he was frightened even in the slightest, he didn't show it.

"That would be me." Ashley held out her hand to him with a smirk on her lips.

Ibrahim declined her offer of a handshake. "Good. I wish to talk privately with you. The temple will be a good place, I think."

Ashley eyed him. "Why has the Ageless sent you here in her place? I'm accustomed to dealing with her directly."

"She asks for your forgiveness. She has been very much preoccupied in dealing with the Hawks. They've been growing more and more demanding these days. In fact, that's what I'm here to talk to you about. But, due to the sensitive nature of the subject, I would like some privacy first and foremost."

As soon as Ibrahim mentioned the Hawks, Ashley's face twitched. "Very well," she said. "This had better be worth my time."

Ibrahim and Ashley made their way toward the entrance of the temple and soon disappeared from sight through the wooden doors, swinging them shut behind them. As soon as they had done so, one of the warlocks a few feet away from me whispered "Now!" and the elderly witch tugged on my shoulder.

We all rushed out from our hiding places. The remaining vampires by the fountain were shocked enough to stand rooted to the spot for a few seconds before chasing after us. But by the time they'd caught up, it was too late. We'd formed a circle around the temple and the witches had begun to recite their magic, uttering a low chant. Just as the vampires closed in around us, little Abby heading straight for me, an invisible force field shot up around the temple. As soon as the vessels made contact with it, they were hurled back several feet.

Enraged, they attacked the force field again, their mouths stretched open in what I imagined would have been wild screams. But we heard nothing. The force field, it seemed, also kept out sound.

I stepped back from the circle of witches and neared the entrance of the temple. I was at a loss as to what my role was to be in all of this. I sought out the elderly witch.

"What should I do?" I asked.

"Follow Ibrahim into the temple. But go silently! He will need you when the time comes." Her face twisted in concentration as she focused on keeping the shield intact against the vampires. To my alarm, I now caught sight of a crowd of nearly fifty more vampires emerging from the woods. They must have heard the vessels' screams and come running to assist. The witches were outnumbered. I prayed that they had it in them to sustain their magic long enough for us to complete the mission.

I pushed open the temple's door, sliding inside the dim corridor. Ibrahim and Ashley's voices sounded up ahead. I crept along, closing the distance between us as noiselessly as possible, until I was about ten feet away from the temple's innermost chamber. The pair had already entered it and their shadows bounced off of the stone wall opposite the open door.

"In short, we at The Sanctuary have decided to cut our allegiance with the Hawks and support the Elders in full," Ibrahim explained. "The Hawks have simply been asking too much of us recently. We can no longer cater to their demands. It's reached the point where we cannot remain neutral any longer. We must choose sides, either yours or the Hawks'."

"And what has made you want to choose us?"

"Frankly, we believe that the Hawks are the lesser threat. We'd rather have them as enemies than yourselves. We will create more immunes and continue to allow you access to this realm. We will also put all our efforts into trying to recreate our powers so that we have the ability to manifest new gates, since I'm aware that the Hawks managed to eliminate the gate at The Blood Keep…"

I was so engrossed in their conversation that I failed to notice someone approaching me from behind. By the time I realized, it was too late. I felt a blow to my head and went tumbling to the ground, in full view of the open doorway. A vampire guard towered over me and Ashley's eyes fell on me.

"Derek Novak," Ashley hissed, striding toward me.

From the corner of my eye, I noticed Ibrahim take advantage of the distraction and rush over to a hole in the floor.

I scrambled to my feet and steadied myself. "Yes, that's my name."

Without warning, Ashley's claws shot out and she flew at my throat. I ducked and launched into a sprint down the corridor. I didn't know where I would lead them to, and I was beginning to worry about hitting a dead end. I had no witch to assist me in protecting Ashley. If I was forced to ignite flames to protect myself, I would burn Ashley's body to ashes.

I kept running, leading them round the winding corridors and as far away from Ibrahim as I could. But then it finally happened. I took a wrong turn and hit a dead end. I stretched out my palms and unleashed a billow of fire, hoping that it would scare them back.

It didn't deter them.

Ashley narrowed the space between us until she was but three feet away. I looked at the wreck that barely even resembled Ashley any more and felt a pang of guilt. I'd already dealt her more than her fair share of suffering in the past. I battled with myself over what I was about to do. *Look at her, Derek,* a part of myself reasoned, trying to justify to myself what I now saw as inevitable. *She now looks in a worse state than even Sofia was in.*

Taking advantage of my reluctance to harm its vessel, the Elder reached for my throat and attempted to bite into my flesh. I grabbed Ashley's arms and yanked them away from me. Then I kicked her stomach. She reeled back a few steps.

I lost balance as the guard dove for my right leg and began dragging me away from the corner I'd retreated into. I swung my left leg upward in one sharp motion, smashing it against his jaw. The back of his head collided with the wall.

Having recovered, Ashley flew at me once again, this time managing to dig her fangs into my arm. She was preparing to insert venom into my bloodstream. *Would this venom even turn me? Can I even be turned back to my former state?* It wasn't a risk I was willing to take.

I placed a hand against her neck and released a sharp pulse of heat. Ashley jumped back, squealing and clutching the burn. But, to my dismay, she came for me again.

I'm so sorry, Ashley, I whispered. I looked into her blank eyes, knowing that her soul was trapped somewhere behind them. I inhaled and braced myself for the release of a flame that she wouldn't survive.

Her hands outstretched, she aimed for me once more.

But as my fingertips were on the verge of eruption, she halted mid-air and fell to the ground, writhing and howling with pain. Barely a second later, the guard mirrored her behavior. Then they both became motionless.

What in the world...

Ibrahim appeared, sweating and out of breath. He had a gash across his left cheek.

"What..." I began to ask.

"It's destroyed, Derek. I destroyed the gate. The evil spirits who were still on this side of the gate are no longer able to survive Earth's atmosphere without any remaining link connecting back to Cruor. They will soon, or have already, withered away."

"Which means..." I ran back through the corridors until I reached the innermost chamber. Another guard lay on the ground, blood drenching the claws of his right hand; Ibrahim's, no doubt. Where the gate had been, there was no sign that anything other than solid stone floor had ever existed.

I left the chamber and headed toward the outer layer of The Sanctuary until I reached the exit. I yanked the door open and, although the witches still surrounded the temple in a tight circle, the army of vampires who had previously been battling against the shield now lay strewn on the ground.

Seeing that Ibrahim had caught up with me, I asked, "So they're gone? F-forever?" I found it hard to fathom the implications of what we had just accomplished.

"As long as no new gates are created. I don't know if our kind will ever be capable of developing the kind of magic our Ancients wielded in order to create the gates. Once a power like that has been neglected for generations, it's almost impossible to rekindle." Then Ibrahim turned to the witches and said, "You can relinquish the shield now. Our work here is done."

They did as instructed and sounds from the island met my ears again. The screaming had stopped and instead my ears were met with the crash of the distant waves against the shore and the rustling of leaves. It was as though the island itself was sighing with relief.

"So... so that means that..." I was still stumbling over my words and trying to grapple with the situation. "Hawks and Elders... there's no way they can trouble us anymore? We're free?"

Just as I said the words, the Ageless manifested herself in front of the fountain, just a few feet away from us. She looked sternly at me but then fixed her gaze on Ibrahim.

"So, I see you were successful," she said. "And now you understand what remains to be done?"

Ibrahim nodded.

"What?" I asked. "What remains to be done?"

The Ageless ignored me. "You don't have long. I gave you this concession because you are my cousin. But you understand that we must carry out what we agreed upon."

"Concession? What are you talking about?" I tried to grab hold of the witch's shoulder but, to my frustration, the minute I touched her she vanished into thin air. "Damn you!" I yelled at the empty space that only seconds before had been occupied.

I faced Ibrahim. "Well? Explain."

"I will, Derek. But first, I suggest we bring your friends and family here to The Shade. The Elders are no more, and I believe it's the safest place for now. My companions here will start to care for the vessels."

An unnerving feeling began to creep over me and Ibrahim's unwillingness to discuss it only served to further fuel the fire of my doubts.

We've wiped out the gates of the Hawks and Elders, but what kind of evil are we now left with?

CHAPTER 31: SOFIA

Ibrahim didn't even give me a chance to say goodbye to Derek. For all I knew, it could be the last time I saw him. The whole island had been transformed into a hive of wasps. I shuddered to think of what could happen on his arrival.

But there was nothing I could do other than wait and hope for the best. It took me almost an hour after Derek's sudden disappearance to compose myself enough to speak to anybody. Zinnia and Gavin respected my silence and left the room, muttering about going out to look for some animal blood for us.

Then I made my way back upstairs to see if Vivienne had woken yet. I'd been meaning to speak to her since we first rescued her from the ship, but she had seemed to be in no state to talk to anyone.

I knocked on her bedroom door, and when there was no answer, I entered anyway. She lay in bed, eyes open and staring blankly at the ceiling. It was only when I sat on the bed next to her that she turned her head to face me.

"Sofia," she said hoarsely, reaching for my hand. She looked at me differently now than when I'd had an Elder inside me; I guessed that she had already sensed that I was my old self again, save for the fact that I was still a vampire. "What happened to you?" she asked.

I explained about the time I'd spent under the Elder's influence. But the real reason I'd come to see her, and what I truly was dying to do, was to offer an apology.

"Vivienne, when I visited you in your room at Headquarters and told you about... about Xavier. I'm so sorry. I don't even know for a fact that the words I spoke were true, since I didn't witness his death with my own eyes. Everything I said came directly from the Elder's mouth."

She cast her eyes away from me and gulped. She looked on the verge of tears again, but she swallowed her emotions back. "It's okay, Sofia. You weren't in control of yourself. How can I blame you for that? And in any case... I-I think it's about time that I come to terms with the fact that I'm not going to see him again. It'll be less painful in the long term."

I held her in my arms and kissed her forehead, running one hand through her hair. There was nothing I could say that wouldn't make her feel worse, for her conclusion was the truth.

Eventually she broke the silence and asked, "Where's Derek?"

I didn't want to lay any extra worries on my sister-in-law's shoulders. "Ibrahim took him to meet the Ageless," I lied. "I'm not sure what for exactly, because he left very suddenly. But he should be back within a day or so."

After I'd spent a couple of hours with Vivienne, I left her alone and went downstairs to see if Gavin and Zinnia had returned. Indeed they had, but instead of the sacks of blood that we were used to at Headquarters, they'd bought hunks of raw meat and bags full of fresh fish from the local shops.

"There's not much blood in the meat, but you'll have to make do for now," Zinnia said.

"Seems like the dog is asking for breakfast," Gavin muttered, as howling started in the basement. Shadow must have woken up and smelt the dead flesh. "I'll go feed him."

It wasn't long before the two couples came down to join us, closely followed by Eli and Landis. We all sat around the large kitchen table and began tucking into our meal. All the vampires ate hungrily while I pecked here and there just for the sake of normalcy. Gavin and Zinnia settled for cereal they'd picked up from the grocery store.

I repeated much of the conversation I'd just had with Vivienne, an overview of everything that had happened since I last saw them. And again I lied about Derek when they asked where he had gone.

Craving solitude, I grabbed some fish for Vivienne and brought it up to her on a tray. Then I left for my own room and spent the rest of the daylight hours in bed. It was too much for me to keep engaging in conversations with people who were oblivious to the fact that my husband was in mortal danger.

Just as the sun was setting and I was preparing myself to spend a night alone in bed, there was a soft rapping at the door and to my delight, Derek entered.

His face had gained a few new scars and his arms looked cut up and bloody, but other than that, I couldn't complain about the state he'd been returned to me in. He had survived. That was all I cared about.

I flung myself against him, winding my legs around his waist. His body was still sweaty from battle. Before I could start asking questions, he said, "We did it. We ruined the gates. The Elders are gone, forever."

I lowered myself to the ground and my first instinct was to breathe out a sigh of relief. But something was off. Why wasn't he smiling down at me, instead of furrowing his brows and chewing on his lower lip?

"Why aren't you happy?"

"The witches," he muttered. "They haven't destroyed their gates yet. Something is up. Ibrahim has promised to shed more light on the matter once we've returned to The Shade."

Return to The Shade. I couldn't keep the excitement from bubbling up within me at the thought of returning home. Yet, at the same time, I was filled with dread at the state we might find it in. I had no idea how many had survived, or how many we had lost.

"And Rose," I said. "Will it be safe to have Corrine return with Rose?"

"I would rather that we wait until I understand better what twisted plans are going on in the mind of that bitch. For now, let's just gather everyone up here and return. I already met Gavin and Zinnia on my way up here and they've started alerting the others."

Within five minutes, everyone stood around the kitchen table, except Shadow and Ibrahim who were on top of it.

"Lock arms," Ibrahim ordered. Once we were all touching each other, he began reciting a chant. He placed one hand on Derek's shoulder and the other on Shadow's back. As soon as he made contact, his magic rushed through us. Violent wind blew against me and I was forced to shut my eyes. When I reopened them, I was met with the sight of The Shade's Port. A salty breeze wafted past and the fresh scent of trees filled my nostrils.

We were home.

CHAPTER 32: SOFIA

None of us spoke a word. I knew all of us shared the anxious feeling in the pit of my stomach. After the Elders' conversation about what they'd been doing to the humans and vessels, I felt scared about what I might lay eyes on each time we turned a corner.

What if there are no humans or vessels left? What if they already took them all back to Cruor?

We walked through the forest until we reached the clearing just in front of the Sanctuary. Vivienne was the first to rush forward and examine the bodies lying on the ground. Most of these vampires I did not know the names of, but then I saw a little familiar figure lying on the ground. The witches who had accompanied Derek there were all huddled around the vampires, nursing them back to health. I was relieved to see Abby lying on the lap of an elderly witch, her eyes open, despite looking exhausted.

"Where's Ashley?" Derek asked one of the witches. "You know, the female vampire the head Elder had possessed."

"She must still be in the temple," the witch said. "We haven't reached the bodies in there yet, there have been so many out here to deal with."

"Take me to her!" I said, grabbing hold of Derek and pulling him in the direction of the temple. He led me along a corridor toward the center of the building until we reached a passageway where a wrecked Ashley lay sprawled on the floor. Beside her was a vampire guard, also unconscious and in a similar condition.

Derek picked Ashley up and said, "Let's bring her outside. I'll send someone back here to take care of the guards."

We moved toward the exit but when we passed the entrance to the innermost chamber, I called out to Derek, "Go on without me, I'll catch up with you."

I recalled that this chamber had been the last place I'd laid eyes on Xavier. I walked from one end to the other and all around the edges of the room just to check I hadn't missed his body concealed in any shadows. But he was indeed gone. It pained me beyond measure that Vivienne wouldn't even have his body to bury.

By the time I'd exited the temple, two witches were already bent over Ashley. They examined her closely.

"What are her chances?" I asked in a hushed tone.

"She's a few hundred breaths away from death," a witch said. I crouched beside them and watched with bated breath as they worked their magic.

"Derek! Sofia!" Zinnia's shrill voice echoed through the courtyard. I looked around to see her and Gavin rushing toward us. "We need you at the Cells *now*! Hurry!"

I felt torn between leaving Ashley or going to aid Zinnia and Gavin. I looked up at the two witches and knew that she was in capable hands. My watching over her wouldn't have any impact over whether she lived or died.

I grabbed Derek's hand and we followed Zinnia and Gavin through the woods. Gavin ended up jumping onto Derek's back and Zinnia onto mine, since even with their weights on our backs, we could still run ten times faster than either of them on their human legs.

When we arrived outside the entrance to the Black Heights, Gavin and Zinnia slid off of us and pushed open the creaking door. The smell of damp and decay flooded over us. I remembered what it was like to walk through the Cells all those days ago, the conditions our people were living in. But now, as I looked around, I realized it had become many times worse.

"There are just so many humans and vampires locked up here, we need your help urgently. Many are sick and even more are on the verge of death from lack of water and food," Gavin said.

Derek reached up toward a high shelf near the entrance and pulled down about two dozen keys. He handed a set to me and said, "Most of the locks take the same key. You'll have to experiment until you find the right one. We need to get them out of this hellhole and into the fresh air outside. Gavin and Zinnia—Sofia and I will work on releasing everyone from the Cells, but you're in charge of herding them all outside and organizing them."

My hands shook as I began opening the locks. Shouts and cries of joy met my ears when they saw what I was doing. They came rushing out and many children latched onto me and hugged me. But I couldn't stay long with any of them and instead directed them toward Zinnia and Gavin, for Derek and I still had a long night ahead of us.

There were some humans who were no longer able to walk, or who had passed out, and occasionally some dead. Derek and I carried out all the survivors and placed them on the soft grass outside the door of the mountain, beneath the clear night's sky.

After several hours, we'd managed to clear out all the humans. Next were the vampires. Many of them were in just as bad a state as the humans, lying on the floor with injuries and deprived of blood for God knows how long. We assembled them a few meters away from the humans. Those who were still in a reasonably healthy state were instructed to fetch emergency supplies—animal blood for the vampires, water and bread for the humans.

Once we were certain there was nobody left behind in the dungeons, Derek and I exited the mountain range and looked around the clearing, surveying the countless people lying on the ground and the remaining milling about offering assistance.

Just as we were about to enter the crowds to begin helping ourselves, loud barks echoed down from the rocks above. Thirty black vampire mutts dashed down from the boulders. Their red eyes glinting and sharp fangs bared, it was clear what these dogs were. *Angry. Hungry. Racing toward warm human blood.*

"Derek!" I gasped.

But he had already noticed. He took off running full speed toward the spot they were descending to. I followed him, baring my claws.

Just as the dogs were landing on the ground, Derek stretched out his palms and fire blazed from them, engulfing the dogs with flames. They barked and whimpered in shock and pain. Dozens fell to the grass, dead. But three had used the smoky haze as an opportunity to take a detour around us. They had climbed all the way to a different side of the mountain, about twenty feet away from us, and were about to rush toward the humans from that angle.

"No!" I screamed. I flew forward and cut deep gashes into two of the dogs' necks with my claws, slicing through their arteries. But one managed to escape me. I heard screams and looked around wildly to see it about to leap into the helpless crowd.

In a whirl of black clashing with black, Shadow emerged from the crowd. He knocked the dog to the ground and ripped into its neck, Eli racing close behind him. Shadow didn't let go of the dog until he'd completely torn its throat out. Then he dragged the body away from the humans, leaving a bloody trail on the grass behind him, and dropped it directly on top of my feet.

"Thank you, boy," I said, scratching his ear as I pulled my feet out from beneath the corpse. I wiped the blood from my hands on the grass and walked over to Derek.

"Good job," he said, a hint of amusement creeping over his face. "I still haven't gotten used to you being a vampire."

"Well, start getting used to it." The idea of finding a cure for myself still seemed far off.

We walked back toward the humans and spotted Ibrahim emerging from the woods, several witches by his side. They dispersed into the crowd and started attending to the sick. Wiping the sweat from his brow, Derek looked at them with gratitude. We walked over to Ibrahim and Derek asked, "Why are you doing this? What has helping us got to do with your council's orders?"

"Not a lot, I'm afraid," Ibrahim sighed. "But not all of us agree with the Ageless and the council's way of doing things any more. And besides, we're following all their major orders. They're not here to see us helping the weak and elderly, so why not use our skills to do something good for a change?"

Derek seemed speechless. "So you're going against your council's orders by offering medical assistance?"

"Let's just say that it wasn't specified in the job description."

"So you're not all as heartless as I thought."

"I'm not completely devoid of self-interest. I... I'm not sure that Corrine would ever forgive me if I didn't do all within my power to help you in this hour of need... and I very much seek her approval of me." Ibrahim blushed slightly.

"Well"—Derek cleared his throat—"whatever your motivation, thank you for your assistance."

"I'm sure you'd agree it's the least we can do," Ibrahim replied.

"But now, tell me what's the deal. You've helped wipe out the gates to Cruor and Aviary. The Elders and Hawks are no longer in this realm." Derek looked him dead in the eye. "I've been kept in the dark long enough. What was the witch talking about? What concession? And what does your kind have in store for us next?"

Ibrahim put an arm around Derek's shoulder and started speaking in a quieter tone of voice. "See, that's the thing, Derek," he said. "We *haven't* ruined all the gates yet."

My gut clenched.

"What? Oh, no. You're saying that the Elders and Hawks have more than three gates each?"

"No," Ibrahim said. "That's not what I'm saying. I'm saying that one of the six gates hasn't been obliterated yet. A gate still exists in Headquarters."

Chapter 33: Derek

"What? No, Ibrahim. You don't know what you're talking about. I saw the Ageless…" I stuttered.

"Ah, but *did* you see?" Ibrahim interrupted. "Because it looked to me like you walked out of that chamber before you actually saw the Ageless eliminate the gate."

"Huh?"

"I witnessed the scene back at Headquarters, Derek. I arrived shortly after the Elder was expelled from Sofia's body. You just didn't notice me watching from the shadows. But I saw it all… the despair in your eyes when you begged the Ageless for a chance to search for your son."

His words knocked the wind right out of me. My mouth opened and closed. Sofia grasped my arm, a similar expression on her pale face.

"I know how much family means to you," Ibrahim continued. "Hell, I hope to have my own family one day. I knew what you must have been feeling when the witch refused to allow you enough time to pursue the only clue you have about your baby's whereabouts. Also... your little Rose... I'll admit that she's grown on me during the time I've spent watching over her. I'd hate to see her grow up without her brother."

"So you..."

"Yes," Ibrahim said. "Before the Ageless could finish her spell and seal the gate forever, I persuaded her to reconsider her stance. We are blood relations and my words mean something to her, even despite the influence the council has on her. I told her that if she wanted *my* continued cooperation, something she does place value in, then she would strike a deal with me: keep the last gate open until you helped me destroy the final gate to Cruor, and then allow you a maximum of twelve hours to go through and search for your family. I arranged for five witches to stand by the gate to make sure no Hawks come back through into this realm in the meantime."

"And now..."

"Despite what I have said, it is imperative that you understand the risks, Derek. Don't let your emotions cloud your judgment. The odds of you being successful, or even surviving the visit, are very, very slim. Neither I nor any of the witches can accompany you; our powers are futile in Aviary. The same goes for your fire. You will have no power once you are there. There's only a very rare kind of witch whose powers work in Aviary, and we don't have access to any such person. So you will be all alone." Ibrahim's eyes bored into mine. "I want Rose's brother back, but I also don't want her to lose her father. Consider your next move wisely. I'll give you an hour to make your decision. If you decide to take up the risk, we'll leave for Headquarters together. But if, however, you decide to forego the risk, I'll return to Headquarters alone and destroy the gate. The patience of the Ageless wears thin."

With that, Ibrahim turned on his heels and made his way back toward the direction of the witch's temple.

Sofia and I stared blankly at each other for several minutes. Eventually it was Sofia who broke the silence.

"Derek," she croaked, "what confuses me is that we keep imagining our son being in Aviary, but it makes no sense. How on earth would he have gotten there? We seem to be forgetting that it was Kiev who kidnapped him. Not one of the Hawks. Our hunt for him there could turn out to be some wild goose chase."

"I know. I know. But it's all we have. Also we do know that your father is there, along with Ian, Anna and Kyle."

"Barely a moment has passed that I don't think of them. But if we're considering this—undertaking this gargantuan task within the span of twelve hours—we need to be laser-focused on who our actual target is. We may not have time to look for everyone..." Her voice broke off.

"I know. I know." I rubbed my fingers over my eyes, wondering if I was mad to even consider doing this. "I don't know why you keep saying 'we', Sofia. There will be no 'we'. Only myself. We can't run the risk of Rose losing both of her parents in one fell swoop."

"No." Sofia started shaking. "I can't let you do this alone. You will have no powers there. No chance of surviving even a minor attack. At least I'll have my fangs and claws. If you decide to do this, I'm coming with you."

"But Rose! We can't..."

"And I can't let you go alone. The chances of you surviving on your own are probably half of what they would be if I accompanied you. You going alone risks your life and that of our son... if we really think he's there somewhere. Rose is safe with Corrine and Ibrahim."

My mind was so jumbled I didn't know what to think anymore. I leaned against a rock and slid down to the floor, placing my head against my knees. Sofia slid down next to me.

I was aware of the minutes passing by. Our hour would soon be up.

"I don't know that I could stand living such a life of regret. If we let the gate disappear... knowing it could have been in my power to save my father or son..." Sofia murmured. "The thought of risking Rose growing up without us slices my heart in two. But I know Corrine and Ibrahim would be good parents to her. Corrine's already become more of a mother to her than I am."

I wrapped my arms around Sofia and pulled her close to me, staring intensely into her green eyes that were several shades more vibrant now that she was a vampire. *Do we really want to take this risk, Sofia? What if only one of us survived? What if I lost you?* I'd already experienced losing Sofia more than my fair share of times and it was an experience I had no desire to repeat.

Suddenly her face lit up. "What if Ibrahim put a spell on us before we went through the gate? What if he gave us the appearance of Hawks? Surely that would lessen our risk?"

"What if the spell wore off the moment we entered Aviary? He already said his powers aren't effective there."

Sofia caught hold of my hand and pulled me up. She tugged on me to start following her away from the clearing and back through the woods. We didn't stop until we'd reached the temple where Ibrahim sat alone in the moonlight by the fountain.

"If you put a spell on us before we entered the gate and made us look like Hawks, would it last once we reached Aviary?"

Ibrahim raised his eyebrows, and then frowned. "If we cast the spell before you entered the gate, then in theory our magic should remain intact at least for a few hours. I say in theory because we've never tried such an experiment. Worst-case scenario, you'd risk your disguise rubbing off before you managed to complete your mission."

Sofia looked up at me, eyes blazing. "Well, we'd be better off with that. We could better hide ourselves and even be stronger, and we'd have the advantage of flight…"

"No, you wouldn't," Ibrahim said. "We can give you the *appearance* of a Hawk. But we're not skilled enough to give you the strength and powers of a Hawk. Our spell would be useful for disguise purposes only."

"Well, we'd still be better off. If the spell lasted long enough, nobody would know we weren't Hawks."

A silence followed for at least several more minutes as we considered Sofia's proposal.

"Are you sure about this? You've considered that we may…" I said.

"Yes. I've considered all sides of this situation. I won't be able to live with myself if we don't at least try. At least the risks aren't as high if Ibrahim puts this camouflage spell on us."

Ibrahim raised his eyebrow again at this last assumption of Sofia's, but he remained silent, allowing us to come to our final decision without his influence.

"We could give ourselves four hours," she continued, "four hours to get at least a hint of where our son or Aiden or Ian, Anna and Kyle could be situated. If we've had not even the faintest hint where to even start looking after four hours, we'll consider returning back through the gate. I-I just can't sit here and not at least try to do something, Derek!"

I looked across the courtyard, now completely cleared of bodies. There was no sign of Ashley or what had become of her. Vivienne lurked around the entrance of the temple. Her shoulders sagged as she looked around. To my dismay, she caught my eye and cocked her head in question. I didn't want her knowing what we were about to do. She had enough troubles to bear as it was. Knowing that she might be about to lose the last close member of her family, her twin brother, was too much for me to inflict on her.

So I just gazed back at her silently, trying to keep my expression blank. Although as my twin, she could probably feel my anguish bubbling up within her own stomach. She would know something was wrong, just not what.

"All right," I muttered beneath my breath. "Let's try."

The moment I said the words and Sofia nodded her head in agreement, Ibrahim's hand clamped on my shoulder. Then Vivienne's form along with the rest of The Shade vanished into a blur of colors.

CHAPTER 34: SOFIA

Back in the circular chamber at Headquarters, Ibrahim and three other witches stood around Derek and I. The others had agreed to join in on a spell in an attempt to make our camouflage last longer.

"Close your eyes," Ibrahim said.

We did as we were told and Derek's hand clasped mine. And then their chant started. Softly at first, but gradually growing louder and louder, words I could not recognize, but that sounded precise and sharp nonetheless, some powerful ancient tongue.

I expected pain as my physical features transformed. But I felt nothing. And when the ritual came to an end, I wondered if they'd failed.

But then I let go of Derek's hand and placed both hands on my face. Sure enough, where my nose and mouth had been was a sharp bump. The shape of a beak. Tough leathery wings had sprouted just beneath my shoulder blades. I turned to look at Derek and despite the situation almost laughed. He too had transformed into an overgrown bird.

We cast our eyes down into the starry abyss, the pale blue whirling substance forming the walls of the tunnel.

"So now we just… jump?" Derek asked.

"Yes. This will lead you directly to Aviary. You'd better hope no Hawks are watching this gate at the other end. If there are, I suggest you jump right back through again."

Derek and I exchanged nervous glances.

"And remember… I can't promise you I'll be able to keep this open more than twelve hours. I will do my best, but if the Ageless enforces her will, there's not much I can do. Just make sure you're back within plenty of time."

Derek took a deep breath and jumped first. His body shot downward through the tunnel and disappeared from sight. Fastening my hair in a bun, I took the leap myself.

As soon as I fell, the suction swallowed me down. I was travelling at such a speed that everything was a haze. I could barely breathe and my heartbeat tripled its pace.

Just as it felt like I was about to pass out, the tunnel came to an abrupt end and I was thrown upward, landing on a bed of leaves. Rubbing my head, I dared to open my eyes. The sweltering heat settled over my skin. The sticky, humid atmosphere did nothing to help me catch my breath. I'd landed a few feet away from Derek. We didn't have much time to gather our wits about us. Our first priority was to make sure that we were alone.

Derek crept through the undergrowth and ducked down next to me. We were sitting in some kind of jungle. Brightly colored insects the size of bats buzzed around us. The chattering and cawing of exotic birds filled the atmosphere. The air smelled of rich pollen. And it was strangely dark. I looked up to see a dense canopy of sharp-edged leaves.

Beads of sweat were already breaking out on my forehead.

"What is this place?" I breathed out.

Derek was still looking around us. "We're alone." He lifted himself up from our hiding place, standing on his tiptoes. "Too bad these wings are useless," he said. "I have no idea which direction we should even start heading for. And we can't afford to waste any time."

I joined him in standing up and looked around. We could barely see twenty meters; the jungle vegetation was dense and the patches of fog didn't help either.

"Well, let's first get away from this gate. It's not a good idea to hang around here. I'm shocked it wasn't guarded in the first place," I muttered. "Let's try climbing to the top of a tree to see if we can get a better idea of where we should be headed."

Derek caught my hand and we began walking toward a tree with low-hanging branches. He grabbed hold of one and hauled himself up, then extended his hand. I refused his help. I had enough strength to do my own climbing.

As we ascended one close-knit layer of leaves at a time, careful not to lose our footing on the moist bark, it was becoming lighter and lighter. The air also felt more oxygenated; I was beginning to breathe more freely.

Then a moss-covered tree branch began moving. It was a colossal snake, heavier than any I'd ever seen in my life. I nearly screamed as it lifted its head and began hissing at me. Derek, who had already climbed up to a branch just above me, reached down and yanked me up. We quickened our climbing, hoping the snake wouldn't follow us. I tried to ignore the spiders twice the width of my hand that scuttled along the branches inches away from my feet, and the shiny foot-long centipedes. It was starting to feel like we'd never reach the top when I heard voices overhead.

Derek and I froze.

A figure dropped down through the layer of leaves above us and balanced himself on the same long branch we were perched on. A male Hawk.

His beak opened in surprise, then he squinted his eyes at us. "What are you doing down here in the Lower Layers? Didn't you hear that orders are for all able Hawks in this quarter to gather in the Battalion for briefings?"

"Briefings…" I said, as though I had any clue what he was talking about. "Yes, of course we heard. How could we not? We're on our way. We were just…" My mind worked furiously trying to concoct some excuse a Hawk might come up with.

Luckily the Hawk was too impatient to hear me out, thus saving me from myself.

"Spare me your excuses and just get a move on!" he growled.

Then he took a leap further downward and disappeared through the canopy of leaves beneath us. Derek breathed out in relief and we continued our climb upward.

Sounds of a civilization started trickling down through the leaves: the distant chattering of hundreds of people all at once, ropes creaking, feet thudding against wood, doors slamming, water splashing. The sounds were getting closer and closer until eventually we poked our heads through a final layer of leaves.

My breath hitched and Derek also inhaled sharply as we gazed around.

"Whoa," I whispered.

By the looks of it, we had climbed up only about a third of the tree. The giant leaves had been stripped away from the trees to create an open space, open enough to build wooden constructions around the tree trunks, interconnected by bridges and walkways. The trunks were now bare from the point we were standing for about three hundred feet upward, where the leaves began again, creating an enclosed area for this wondrous city and forming a ceiling that protected it from the direct heat of the sun.

As for the width of this place, I couldn't begin to estimate. The clusters of magnificent architecture—tree houses small and large, round and square—stretched out for as far as I could see.

A true city in the trees. The Shade has nothing on this.

Dozens of humans walked along various bridges and walkways. But I was struck by the lack of Hawks.

I was about to hoist myself up onto the bridge about five feet above us, but Derek held me back.

"Wait," he whispered. "We need some way to remember this place. Otherwise how will we find our way back here?"

He had a point. I turned my face up toward the leafy ceiling of the city to see if there was anything striking that could serve as a landmark.

"Look!" Derek said. "That carving there, do you see it?"

One of the trees had been cut shorter than the others. Carved into the bark was a striking depiction of a Hawk. I hoped that there was only one such carving.

"All right, now let's go," I said.

We both pulled ourselves up onto the narrow bridge, trying to keep our heads down and not be noticed. The walkway swayed unnervingly as we walked along it. I dared not try to estimate how many feet we might be above the jungle floor. I kept my eyes straight ahead.

At the end of the bridge was a wide platform. Its floorboards spanned the width of a dozen trunks. We had reached a cluster of some of the smaller tree houses. Derek nudged me and pointed to a human girl who'd just entered a construction ten feet away from us.

She'd left the door ajar. We walked over and Derek dared to peek his head inside. He pushed it open further and beckoned me inside. The stuffy room we entered was bare save for primitive cooking facilities and a stained mattress. The girl sat in the corner mending some clothes. She almost jumped out of her skin when we loomed overhead.

"Shhh. It's okay. We're not going to hurt you." I held up my hands as a sign of peace. "I'd just like to ask you, is there a particular place that human recruits are brought to?" She looked at me with fear and confusion. I coughed, realizing I needed to play my role better. "You know, when us Hawks take you away from your homes in the mortal realm, is there any particular place you are gathered?"

"Mama!" she called, getting up and rushing into a room at the back of the building.

A blonde woman who looked to be in her mid-thirties came rushing out. "What do you want?" she asked.

I repeated my question. She cocked her head warily. "Why are you asking me that? You should know better than I."

"Just answer her question, will you?" Derek took a step forward.

"There is no particular place." She scowled. "We're shoved into little boxes like these wherever there's space." With that, she grabbed her child and retreated into the back room.

"Where do we start?" I turned to look at Derek. "There are thousands of these tree houses."

"I don't know. Let me think." Derek scratched the back of his head. We stepped out of the tiny tree house back onto the bridge.

"What are you two *still* doing here?" a voice boomed from behind us.

I whirled around and there stood the same Hawk we had met back down in the "Lower Layers".

"Follow me," he ordered. Derek and I could think of nothing else to do but obey his command. I thanked the heavens that the Hawk didn't immediately take flight and expect us to follow him by air. Instead, he walked. We followed in silence, not daring to say a word. We passed along one shaky walkway after another, past hundreds more tree houses identical to the one we had just visited.

After what felt like half an hour of walking, the little tree houses were becoming fewer and fewer and being replaced by the larger constructions. We stopped outside a massive oval construction, a trunk of a tree running right through the middle of it. We stepped through the entrance and found ourselves in some kind of auditorium. Rows upon rows of Hawks were seated on platforms that covered the rounded walls from top to bottom.

So this must be the Battalion.

Without a word, our escort closed the door on us.

It was dark inside save for bright lights that shone down on a raised platform in the center, where two Hawks addressed the packed audience.

"… And we should expect that their first point of refuge will be the volcanoes."

"Indeed. But this time, we shall not let them within even fifteen miles of them…"

The voice of the second Hawk sent goose bumps running along my arms.

Arron.

I tried to open the main door but it wouldn't budge. Any attempt to force it open would attract the unwanted attention of at least fifty

Hawks perched on benches near the entrance.

I looked back at Derek in panic.

We'd better hope to God our disguises hold up. What this Battalion full of Hawks would do to a vampire in their midst...

181

Chapter 35: Derek

Sofia and I were beginning to attract attention with our insistence on standing by the entrance, so we relented and sat down in spare seats as close to the entrance as possible. Sofia trembled beside me and I reached out to grasp her hand, hoping to instill some form of comfort in her.

As Arron continued to address the audience, we ducked down as much as we could without looking strange.

"… And from today, the humans must all be kept strictly contained to their designated area. We can't afford to allow the leeches access to any fuel. As you all know, being near their blood alone, without even tasting it, can serve to strengthen their influence…"

Each Hawk's eyes were glued on the two men on stage. Sofia's eyes widened. She clamped a hand over her mouth.

"Dad!" she breathed.

Sure enough, Aiden was sitting a few rows along from us.

Although he had been transformed into a Hawk, his vibrant eyes and hair that matched Sofia's were unmistakable.

Before I knew what was happening, Sofia slunk out of her seat and, crouching down low, made her way to where Aiden was seated. Her head disappeared from sight as she arrived next to Aiden's seat. Aiden's head swiveled around and his body jolted as though he'd just been electrocuted. His head bent and his mouth moved furiously. Then he composed himself and looked straight ahead as if nothing had happened.

Sofia crept back to me.

"When I tell you to follow me, you follow. Understood?"

"What is happen—"

"Shh."

After ten minutes, Aiden got up from his seat and made his way toward one of the Hawks standing near the entrance. He whispered something into his ear, and the Hawk nodded and opened the door.

"Now!" Sofia hissed. We left the bench and moved discreetly toward the entrance. The Hawk looked confused as to why we were all leaving at the same time, but Aiden seemed to have enough of a position of authority for him to not question it.

As soon as we had stepped outside and the Hawk shut the door behind us, Aiden marched forward without a word. As he walked, he looked around to be sure no Hawks were following us. I was about to open my mouth when Sofia tugged on my hand and gave me a glare.

Aiden led us back along the wooden walkways to the cluster of tree houses we'd stopped by earlier. This time, we travelled much deeper into the cluster. Outside one of the cabins he rapped on the door and a pale human girl with green eyes and black hair opened it. It took me a second to recognize her as Anna. Despite our disguises, she clamped a hand over her mouth to stifle a scream.

"What… Oh my…"

"Just let us in," Aiden growled. Anna stepped aside and allowed us into the tiny living quarters. Sitting on an uncomfortable-looking couch was Kyle.

As soon as we were all safely inside, Sofia rushed to Anna and swept her up into a tight embrace. Kyle stood up and gave me a hug.

"Wow. Good of you to visit us, Derek!" he said with a broad smile.

I turned to Aiden, but he said, "I can't stay here any longer. I can't have Arron noticing my absence. Stay here until I return. I know that we don't have more than a few hours left…"

Sofia rushed to hug him before he could leave. "Don't you dare be late. I can't lose you again," she said.

Aiden nodded curtly and exited the cabin. Then Sofia gazed around the room. "Where's Ian?"

"They housed him in a different place, a few trees away from here," Anna explained. "So, they turned you into Hawks?"

"No." I shook my head. "This is a witch's spell, just a disguise. We don't even know how long it'll last before it wears off and reveals our true forms."

"Aiden filled us in on what's been happening back home over the past few months. And Sofia"—her eyes lit up with an odd excitement—"I have something to show you."

She ran into the back room and came out carrying what appeared to be a rolled-up blanket. But rolled-up blankets didn't move. Rolled-up blankets didn't cry.

Anna handed the bundle to Sofia. A baby boy with green eyes and black hair. Sofia broke out into hysterics and knelt, clutching the baby in her arms.

"Derek, oh, Derek. Am I dreaming? Tell me, am I dreaming?"

I knelt beside her and brushed the hair away from her face, kissing her wet cheek. "You're not dreaming, my love," I whispered. Her eyes were filled with tears of ecstasy as she looked up at me. "It's our baby... our baby boy... Ben."

I'd tried to hold in my own tears in the face of Sofia's breakdown, but when Ben turned his small face to gaze up at me, I couldn't any longer. I pulled Sofia onto my lap and wrapped my arms around hers, so we could both cradle our child simultaneously.

The rest of the world ceased to exist as we sat there, in a bubble of happiness. Kyle and Anna looked on silently.

Eventually I said, "But how? How is Ben here?"

"I really don't know," Anna replied with a shrug. "Soon after I arrived here, they started carrying out blood tests on Kyle and me. But the rest of the time I was given the job of helping out in the humans' medical aid building. I've been working there ever since. Well, one day Aiden of all people came rushing in here. He told us what had been happening back in our realm and also that Arron had revealed to him that his grandson was here in Aviary. How Ben got here I still don't know. I don't know if even Aiden knows that. But anyway, Aiden requested that I take this little baby into my own care before Ben got sent to live with some other human family."

I examined Ben more carefully. He seemed to be in good health.

"You've done a wonderful job with him, Anna. I don't know how I can ever repay you," Sofia choked.

"I've been so worried about making sure he's healthy," Anna continued. "I've never looked after such a young infant before. Fortunately there are a few newborns in nearby trees whose mothers have had milk to spare for your little boy."

Sofia and I fell silent again, relishing our child's quiet breathing, gazing down into his eyes and stroking his soft skin.

It was Kyle's turn to break the silence. "You really must stay here. Things are changing rapidly here for the Hawks. Rumors are that Cruor is planning another attack on Aviary now that all their gates have been ruined…" Kyle paused in confusion, looking at us. "But the gates to Aviary are also supposed to be dismantled. How on earth…?"

"That's a long story, but there's still one gate open," I said. "A gate which will vanish in less than a few hours. If Aiden doesn't return soon, we're going to have to make a move. We can't risk waiting for him."

Sofia shuddered at the thought of leaving her father behind, but nodded, looking down at Ben who was now drifting off to sleep in her arms.

Anna's eyes widened and she turned to Kyle. "If we're all going to attempt an escape, I need to bring Ian here."

"Be careful, Anna," Kyle said. "Humans aren't supposed to be wandering outside right now while their meeting is going on."

Kyle wrapped his arms around Anna and kissed her before she left. Then he turned back to us and pointed to the door leading to the back of the cabin. "I suggest you stay back there for now." He led us through into an even smaller room with a single mattress on the floor and a tall window. The window had no glass, just meshing to keep out insects. I peeked out of the window and saw a drop of possibly twenty meters down to the floor of leaves below.

Sofia sat cross-legged on the mattress and laid Ben on her lap. Kyle went back into the main room to keep an eye on the front door. Thankfully, Anna wasn't long. We were only waiting for ten minutes before she came through the door with Ian. Like Kyle and Anna, he too was still in human form.

Once Anna had seen him into the room, she went back into the front room with Kyle. Ian bent down to give Sofia a hug, and then placed his hand on my shoulder.

"Well, Anna just filled me in. All I can say is, I've never been happier to see a Novak in my life."

He took a seat next to Sofia and they began talking. I continued to pace up and down the small room, too anxious and aware of the passing time to pay attention to their words. I prayed that Ibrahim would keep his word and not destroy the gate any earlier. And I prayed the Ageless wouldn't try to interfere.

I was beginning to drive myself mad contemplating all the things that could go wrong, so I asked a question.

"Ian, maybe you can answer this. Arron previously spoke of using humans as vessels. Just like when he was back in our realm, his form was different to his Hawk form. Was he inhabiting a human body?"

"Funny, that's a question I asked my roommate myself soon after I arrived. See, Hawks don't use 'vessels' the same way Elders do for the simple reason that Elders don't have any physical body of their own, whereas the Hawks do. So it's incredibly easy for an Elder to enter a vessel—they just seep in. But Hawks can't do that. So, when they want to go to Earth and need a disguise, there are witches here who can morph them into a human's likeness. But in order for that spell to work, they need to bring the humans to Aviary. Witches then use the human's genetics to morph the Hawk's appearance to be exactly like the human's."

"In other words, the human Arron's looks actually belong to a real human who's kept here in Aviary? And Hawks can be made to look like any human, male or female, so long as that human is present here in this realm for their witches to gain access to?"

"That's basically how it works. Unlike the Elders, it's not natural for Hawks to inhabit a human body."

"Then what about Aiden? How is it possible for humans to turn into Hawks?" I asked.

"Again, they have witches here who can do that. But in order for a human to turn, he or she has to actually be in Aviary…"

A banging at the door suddenly interrupted Ian. Sofia looked up with eagerness in her face.

"Yes! That must be Aiden."

She was about to get up and open the door to greet her father when a voice that was decidedly *not* Aiden's began shouting in the front room. My heart leapt into my throat as I grabbed her arm and held her back.

I looked feverishly around the room. My eyes settled on the window. With one pull, I separated the mesh from the window. Then, with shaking hands, I grabbed a blanket from the bed and wrapped it around my chest to form a carrier. I took Ben from Sofia's arms and fastened him in.

"What are you talking about?" Anna had started screaming. "Are you mad? Of course not!"

"We've no choice but to jump," I whispered.

"But we'll never survive that fall!" Ian said hoarsely.

"We have to try. I'll go down first with Ben. I'll better be able to help catch you two that way," I said.

"The others!" Sofia gasped.

The door to our room began to rattle. There was time left for neither talk nor doubt. I lowered myself out of the window, and, trying to at least land on a branch, I let myself go.

Black flashed beneath me. The next thing I knew, I was hanging in the air, one arm supporting Ben, and the other clutched by a Hawk. For a second I feared that looking up would bring me face to face with Arron.

But then Aiden's voice reassured me.

"Climb up onto my back! Hurry!"

He helped me get into a secure position on his back as I used all my strength and agility to avoid crushing Ben beneath my weight. Then he called through the window. "Sofia! Jump!"

Sofia leapt into his arms and clung to his chest. Despite our weight, Aiden's heavy wings remained steady.

At that moment, another Hawk appeared beside us, hovering at our level outside the window. I feared again that it was Arron. I yelled but Aiden interrupted me: "It's all right. This is Rufus. He's a rebel and he's with me. Ian, jump on his back now!"

"I can't leave Anna back there!" Ian shouted.

Just as he spoke, Anna and Kyle came bursting into the room, only just managing to slam and lock the door before Arron squeezed in after them.

All three of them leapt onto Rufus and then we were all flying up toward the green leafy roof of the city.

"The Hawk carving," I breathed into Aiden's ear. The sudden movement had knocked all the breath out of me and Ben was now crying. "The gate is near that carving."

Aiden nodded but said nothing. I could see that all his concentration was in hurtling forward as fast as his wings could carry us. As we were about to hit the ceiling, Aiden shouted, "I'm not going to slow down! Cover the baby and brace yourselves!"

I curved myself around Ben as we hit the roof, taking all the cuts from sharp leaves and branches against my own body. As soon as we made contact with the canopy, Aiden's wings closed so they wouldn't get torn, but he had already worked up enough momentum for us to shoot through the leaves and appear above the roof. I closed my eyes and hoped Sofia had done the same. Once we were under the heat of the blazing sun, I could barely open them due to the bright light.

Sofia moaned in pain as the rays hit her. *The disguise doesn't protect her from the wrath of the sun.* I hoped Aiden wouldn't keep us flying up there too long.

By the time my eyes had adjusted, Aiden had stretched out his huge wings again and was carrying us forward. I looked behind me and to my relief saw that we had not lost the others.

Barely a few moments had passed when Kyle shouted out, "Arron!"

I turned to look back again and saw Arron had now emerged from beneath the treetops. His eyes had narrowed to slits as he came hurtling toward us with all the speed his mighty wings could muster.

"Hurry!" I shouted to Aiden over Ben's cries.

"I'm going as fast as I can!" Aiden gasped.

Arron had the clear advantage, with no weight to carry but his own. I looked around wildly at the sea of treetops beneath us in hope of spotting the Hawk carving.

"The carving is too short! It won't show among the treetops!" I panted. The ceiling of leaves was far too dense.

A gust of wind blew down on me from above, and to my horror, I realized that Arron had caught up and was now hovering over us. Trying to keep Ben safe with one hand, whilst holding on for dear life with the other, I was incapable of even a feeble attempt at fighting him off.

A pain shot through the nerves in my lower back. I looked up again and saw Arron's talons covered with blood. My blood. The weight of Arron's attack made Aiden falter in the air and for a moment I thought he was about to lose all stability.

He's playing with his prey before the final swoop. Arron positioned himself for another attack. Perhaps this time he would pierce right through my midriff.

Abruptly, Aiden took a nose-dive back down toward the treetops. I closed my eyes and wrapped Ben even tighter against me as we once again made contact with the leaves and branches. As soon as we had made it through the layers of leaves in the ceiling, we reemerged in the open area of the city, Arron popping out from the leaves just a few seconds after us.

"Faster!" I urged.

Initially I didn't know why Aiden had chosen this particular spot to duck back down beneath the leaves, but as we hurtled further downward, I saw it: the carving.

As we reached the first level of the Lower Layers, Aiden let out a scream as he miscalculated a dodge and a branch dug right into his wing. Our dive halted to a violent stop. I was flung against a branch as I struggled to make sure it was my back that landed against the bough rather than Ben. Feeling dizzy, I looked around and saw Sofia hanging from a branch just next to mine. She looked just as out of breath as I felt but she managed to swing herself up to safety.

Then we both looked up. Aiden's wing was caught on a sharp branch. It had pierced right through it, leaving him hanging and writhing.

"No!" Sofia shrieked.

Arron dropped down through the leaves and hovered next to Aiden, laughing at his helpless state.

It was then that I registered the absence of Rufus and his passengers.

"Traitor!" Arron snarled in Aiden's face. "You know what we do to traitors in Aviary, don't you?" He cackled as Aiden struggled more violently. Then he looked down at Sofia and me as we watched helplessly. "But wait there for now." He chuckled. As if Aiden had any choice but to wait. "I'll deal with your insipid family first. It's quite convenient actually. The Hawks will be in need of a hearty dinner after all these long meetings we've been having."

He made his way toward me first, I assumed because he thought I was weakest—carrying a newborn in my arms. But Sofia was having none of it. The moment Arron touched down on the branch, she lunged for him. She swung herself onto his back and gripped her legs around his midriff. Then, to my surprise, sharp claws shot out from her hands. She slid them next to his throat and dug them in a little. Then she opened her mouth and as she tilted her head back, her beak and wings disappeared as fangs emerged. It was as though she was breaking through her disguise by calling upon her weapons.

"One single movement from you, *bird*, and I will dig deep," she growled. I had never witnessed such intensity in Sofia. I was taken aback probably more than Arron.

She was a lioness. A lioness protecting her cub.

Sofia nodded as if to say she had Arron under control. Aiden was still dangling and grunting with pain as he hung from his wing. I began to climb up to assist him when a rustling of leaves caused my heart to pound. What if Arron already contacted other Hawks for backup?

But then Rufus landed on the branch—our three friends still clinging to him. They all had gashes and bruises covering their bodies, but at least they were alive.

Rufus climbed up to Aiden and, holding him by the waist for support, separated his wing from the tree. Aiden groaned as he closed his wing behind him. It hung disjointedly compared to the other one.

"Now what?" I said, looking at Sofia.

Time was slipping through our fingers. I had lost my watch

during the struggle with Arron in the sky and I didn't even know how much time we had left before all hope of escaping this nightmarish place would be gone forever.

It was Rufus who responded while drawing a long curved dagger out of his belt. "Reach the gate. Get out of here before it's too late. Escape forever. And hurry."

"Rufus!" Arron spluttered. "You dare to…"

His voice garbled and then quieted as Sofia applied more pressure. A drop of blood trickled down his throat.

"I told you, no movement. That includes speaking," Sofia said.

"I don't know how long I'll be able to contain him," Rufus continued, "or any other Hawks who might have become aware of all of this commotion…"

"Kyle and Ian," I said, "help Aiden keep up with us. We need to reach the ground as quickly as possible."

With that, Rufus placed his long blade exactly where Sofia had been positioning her claws.

Ben was still crying in my arms. I kissed his forehead, then tightened the blanket around me that I had formed into a carrier for him. We began the climb back down to the jungle floor.

"Careful of the snakes!" Sofia warned, pointing to one hanging about five meters away from us. Aiden groaned and grunted as he made his way down. Even with Ian and Kyle's help, he was slow. Too slow. Anna had climbed onto Sofia's back since she seemed to have sprained an ankle.

The air became steadily moister and the darkness increased as we descended, with less sunlight able to escape through the leaves. It seemed that we had been clambering down for at least an hour, but having no watch, I could not count.

"This journey seems so much longer than when we climbed up,"

Sofia said.

"I know. We have to move faster," I replied.

I almost cried out with relief when my foot finally hit solid ground.

"Shh, it's okay, baby, we're nearly home," I whispered to Ben, who was still expressing his discomfort.

Once everyone had joined me, planting their feet firmly in the undergrowth, Sofia and I led the way toward the gate.

I scanned the area, expecting to see the black hole in the jungle floor we had emerged from. But instead I beheld a vision that should have belonged only in a nightmare.

A tall dark figure.

Long razor-like claws outstretched.

Red eyes glinting in the fading daylight.

Chapter 36: Sofia

Kiev.

A monster I'd hoped to never see again for the rest of my life. I had no idea how he could have survived being in this place as a vampire, or how and why he'd come here with my son, but none of it mattered.

He looked first at my baby cradled in Derek's arms, and then at me. As soon as our eyes met, shivers ran down my spine. I considered that we should just attempt to run right past him and jump through the gate, but with Aiden and Anna injured, and Derek one-handed due to holding Ben, we could be slashed by Kiev's claws if he chose to run at us with his strong muscular build.

"After I went to such pains to bring the infant here, you're just going to take him away? Really? Just like that?" His voice rumbled through the jungle like the beginnings of an earthquake.

"Step aside now and we might just spare you, snake," Derek responded for me.

But Kiev didn't even acknowledge Derek's presence, much less his threat. He took a few slow steps forward, scanning my body as though he was ravishing me from a distance. Then his blood-red eyes settled back on my face.

"So they turned you in the end," he muttered. "You know, Sofia, you're more beautiful than even I had imagined you would be as one of my own kind." His face contorted, as though looking at me was causing him pain.

"You heard my husband. Step aside!" I managed to find my voice. I slid Anna off my back and placed her on the ground, then extended my claws in front of him.

A frantic scream pierced the atmosphere, drifting down from the trees above.

"Run faster! I lost hold of him! Arron is coming! And others are follow—"

I trembled as Rufus' voice cut off midsentence.

Kiev smiled. "But why would I want to do that, darling? If I delayed you just long enough for the Hawks to recapture you all... who knows, I might even be able to convince Arron to give you to me. He'd kill Derek for sure and probably also your father, but I'm sure he'd spare your son, whom we could raise together..."

He began pacing up and down.

"Please! Kiev, please let us go." I resorted to begging. There was no time left to consider matters of dignity.

Leaves rustled overhead and boughs creaked. The Hawks were drawing nearer by the second.

Kiev's eyes were still fixed on me, never wavering. I looked back, willing him to find some speck of mercy in his black hole of a heart.

"You know, I think I could make you happy, Sofia." He continued to indulge in his fantasy, speaking slowly and thoughtfully, as if time was of no value. Then, without warning, he left his guarded position by the gate and walked right up to me, gripping my shoulders and bending down so that his face was within inches of my own.

I struggled against his grip, but I'd become too weak from the sun and the climb to stand a chance against him. He eyed my lips hungrily as he said, "I could even let the others go and just keep you. Maybe you'd be faster at forgiving me that way." He looked around at Derek and the others and nodded toward the direction of the gate. "You're free to go if you wish."

They all remained still, eyeing the gate. Derek couldn't approach Kiev in case Kiev lashed out at Ben. Aiden could barely support his own weight. We were all too worn down to be any match for Kiev.

The Hawks clambering down the trees had come within a few meters of us now. I looked frantically around and screamed at Derek, "Go! Escape with Ben! Just leave, all of you!" I stared at my husband, my eyes begging him to take our son, to keep him safe. His blue irises were wide with terror. "Go, Derek! You fool, stop standing there! LEAVE ME!"

Tears streamed down my cheeks and my vision blurred. I couldn't make out if they had indeed saved themselves, or if any of them still waited stubbornly for me.

"Hurry!" Arron shouted overhead.

"Or… am I a better man than that?" Kiev whispered into my ear.

I blinked rapidly to clear my tears and looked into his deep red irises, wondering if my ears were playing tricks on me. He loosened his grip on one of my shoulders and lifted his hand to my face. He ran his fingers gently against my cheek. Then he pressed his lips against my forehead in a chaste kiss, and let go of me.

I stumbled back, in a state of shock. Despite my orders, neither

Derek nor any of the others had moved yet. But, as soon as I was free from Kiev's grasp, they lunged toward the gate.

We pushed Aiden through first and he disappeared into the strange starlit tunnel, then Anna, then Kyle, Ian, and finally I pushed Derek through. Before I took the leap myself, I turned around one last time to see the Hawks hitting the ground and rushing toward the gate.

I lowered myself into the hole, gripping the edges tightly to fight the suction pulling me down, and looked up at Kiev.

He gazed down at me, his eyes suddenly filled with a sorrow that knocked the breath out of me. He nodded slowly before I let go and hurtled down into the abyss.

Kiev was a mystery I would never unravel.

CHAPTER 37: SOFIA

After I landed on the marble floor, my first instinct was to bellow, "Destroy that gate now!"

I didn't even know whom I was yelling at since I hadn't had a chance to look around the room yet. I sat up and saw Derek lying nearby with Ben held above his chest, and the others scattered around, all still recovering from the fall. Ibrahim and the Ageless stood over us.

They heeded my words and began their spell. Within a minute the marble floor had sealed over, the gate to that nightmarish realm now closed. Forever.

"Thank heavens," Ibrahim breathed out as he turned around to survey us panting, dirty and sweaty.

I scrambled to my feet and rushed over to Derek and my distraught baby. I eased the blanket away from Derek's body and lifted Ben into my arms.

"There, there, darling. Shhh. Mommy's here. Mommy's here

now," I whispered, wiping dirt away from his face and kissing his soft cheeks. I sat cross-legged on the floor and let the tears welling up within me fall. *At last, Mommy's here for you.*

Derek crawled over to me and, wiping my tears, held my face in his hands and kissed me hard. "We did it, Sofia. We did it," he whispered into my ear, a smile creeping across his exhausted face.

"Derek," Ibrahim called from across the room. He was bending over my father's torn wing.

Derek got up and walked over to Ibrahim. Now that Derek's back was turned to me I could see the deep wound in his back inflicted by Arron. His shirt was covered with blood.

I got up and walked over to the corner of the room where the Ageless was standing silently.

"Hey, you," I said, not bothering to show respect she didn't deserve. "Will you help Derek out? He's got a nasty wound on his back."

Before she could answer, I walked over to Derek and, interrupting whatever conversation he'd been having with Ibrahim, I tugged on his shirt and walked him over to the Ageless.

Holding Ben—who had now calmed down considerably—with one hand, I helped Derek out of his shirt with the other. The Ageless looked disdainfully at me, but then heaved a sigh. She ordered Derek to lie down on the floor and began some kind of healing ritual.

Satisfied that Derek was being taken care of, I walked across the room to check on Aiden. He had stopped groaning and the huge tear in his wing seemed to have closed up. He was also sitting upright.

"He's healing up nicely," Ibrahim said.

Aiden beamed on seeing me. I rushed into his arms and he held both Ben and me close to his chest, nuzzling the top of my head with his beak.

"I love you so, so much, my darling," were the only words he could muster through his tears. It was hard to believe that just a few hours ago I'd thought that I would never see my father again. And now here I was, wrapped in his embrace.

"Can I hold him?" Aiden asked, looking down at Ben.

I placed my baby in his arms and Aiden's eyes lit up the way only a proud grandparent's did.

Then I took the opportunity to check on Anna. She sat in a corner, leaning against the wall, clutching her ankle with her hands. Both Kyle and Ian sat next to her, looking concerned. I pulled each of them into a tight hug in turn and said, "Thank you. With all my heart, thank you."

They all smiled at me. Anna brushed a strand of hair away from my face and said, "Oh, stop being so formal, Sofia. You don't need to thank us. We're family."

Chapter 38: Derek

The floor felt uncomfortably cold against my chest. I shivered even more once the witch started her healing. It felt like a hundred needles prickling my wound at once.

"It's done," she said after barely a minute.

The pain had indeed vanished. I ran a hand over my back and felt the skin now smooth where the cut had been. I stood up and looked into the witch's cold eyes. I breathed nervously before asking the question that had haunted me ever since she'd first proposed to help us eliminate the gates back in Costa Rica.

"And what now?"

She paused, her gaze on the ground.

"We leave. And we erase our own gates." She sighed.

"But why? Why wouldn't you want to keep your gates open just in case? If it's true that you're no longer powerful enough to create new gates, then…"

"Aviary and Cruor both know we have our own gates. I wouldn't be surprised if they're not already strategizing how to storm our realm and reenter yours through them. It just makes us even more of a target than we already are."

"And once you've destroyed them, you're all gone forever?" I asked, barely daring to believe.

"Yes. At least, I'm not aware of a single witch in our realm who has retained such powers from our Ancients. It's true that we have grown somewhat complacent over all these years…"

"All these years of piling your troubles onto us poor mortals." I finished her sentence for her.

She cleared her throat and turned to face the opposite direction.

"Ibrahim!" she called. Ibrahim was now bending over Anna and healing her ankle. He left her and walked over to us.

"What?"

"It's time we left. We've dragged out this mission long enough," she said.

Ibrahim looked at her for a moment before saying in a low voice, "I'm not returning with you."

"What?"

"You heard. I'm staying here."

"But, Ibrahim, why? You're my best…" she stuttered.

"The Sanctuary is no longer a place I can consider my home. You and its other residents… I can't see eye to eye with any of you any more."

"But…"

"And besides, Odelia." Ibrahim cut her off again. "I'm in love with Corrine. I… I want to marry her."

The Ageless' brows rose as she gazed at Ibrahim, her mouth agape. I couldn't tell how much of her surprise came from Ibrahim addressing her in public by what I assumed was her real name and how much came from his confession.

The silence lasted for several moments. The Ageless struggled to maintain her composure but couldn't hide a look of hurt that flickered in her eyes.

"Very well," she said eventually. "I see you've made your mind up. In that case, we'll return without you."

"We?" Ibrahim asked.

"Ibrahim, you brought with you a dozen other witches."

"They too wish to stay here. That's why I selected them. Like me, they no longer feel at home with our own kind. That includes my brother, who is now with Corrine," Ibrahim said calmly.

More silence.

Then the Ageless said, "Very well. I'll return alone and wipe out the gates behind me." She placed a hand on Ibrahim's shoulder. "I just hope, cousin, that you won't live to regret this decision."

"I won't," Ibrahim said, not flinching for a second. The Ageless was about to turn away when Ibrahim continued, "Before you leave, you need to restore Corrine's powers—powers that you unjustly took from her."

Before the Ageless could respond, Ibrahim began muttering under his breath and two figures appeared in the room next to him: a tall dark-haired man who strikingly resembled Ibrahim, and Corrine, carrying in her arms a small bundle.

The Ageless nodded. Ibrahim took Rose from Corrine and held the baby while she went and stood directly in front of the Ageless.

The Ageless raised both of her hands in the air and turned her palms toward Corrine. Rays of light shot out of them and hit Corrine, whose whole body jolted back as if hit by electricity. Then the Ageless lowered her hands and said, "Now, I really must leave."

She looked around the room, her eyes lingering on Ibrahim and finally on me. She lingered long enough for me to detect a hint of regret in her cold irises, similar to that which I had noticed back at the beach hut.

And then, without another word, she vanished.

I ran over to Ibrahim as soon as she'd gone and scooped up my beautiful baby daughter.

"Aiden!" I said, excitement rising in my chest. He was still resting on the ground, holding Ben. The look of sheer ecstasy in his eyes when I handed Rose to him so that he was now holding not one, but two, grandchildren in his arms made my heart sing.

"You've just made an old man very, very happy, Derek," he choked.

I realized that this was the first time Rose and Ben had met outside of Sofia's womb. Aiden held them close so that they could face each other. Rose reached out a small hand and touched Ben's nose, her face filled with wide-eyed wonder. A small smile spread from the corners of Ben's lips across his face as he too extended a hand which brushed against Rose's chin.

"I can only hope they grow up to be as close as you are to Vivienne, Derek," Sofia said with tears once again welling in her eyes. She put her hands on my shoulders and drew me in for a passionate kiss.

Vivienne.

Despite the joy I was experiencing, I tensed against Sofia's touch. A surge of guilt hit me, guilt that I should be experiencing such happiness when I knew how intensely Vivienne was suffering.

"So… now what, Derek?" Sofia looked up at me. She seemed to have noticed that she'd touched a raw spot.

"I say it's time we all go home."

CHAPTER 39: SOFIA

If ever The Shade had felt like home, it was now. As we walked away from where Ibrahim and Corrine had made us appear near the temple, Aiden still held Rose and Derek cradled Ben. I looked around at my family, finally all in one place.

We went on a short tour of the island, passing by the remains of the Vale, and then moving toward the Residences. My heart broke when I saw all the beautiful tree houses had now been destroyed—Derek's included—their remains scattered on the forest floor.

"We've got a lot of work to do, Ibrahim," Corrine said, looking around the place.

"It's nothing we can't handle. I'm sure we can restore this island to its original state within a few days. Remember, we have a team of witches here to help us." Ibrahim smiled at her, his arm around her waist as we walked.

"But this time," I said, "we must build proper homes for the humans on the ground. No more stuffing them all into those tiny holes you call rooms in the Catacombs."

"Agreed," Derek said.

"I still think it's a good idea to keep the vampires and humans separated," Kyle said. "Humans on the ground, vampires up in the trees."

"Especially because the time has come for us to finally enforce a ban on human blood," I said. "From now on, all vampires must follow my and Vivienne's example of drinking animal blood."

"Hear, hear!" Ian clapped his hands.

"Well, they're not going to like that," Derek said. "But I agree that we've come too far to go back to our old ways here. It's a very different kingdom we now have the opportunity to build."

"We'll gather the witches and get to work tidying this place up," Ibrahim said. "By now they should have finished healing the sick."

We continued walking to the clearing outside the Black Heights where we had left all the wounded humans and vampires. Sure enough, there was barely anyone lying on the ground. Most had dispersed to whatever remained of their respective homes, I assumed.

Ibrahim and Corrine joined the crowd of witches and they all huddled together and began talking.

"Sofia!" two familiar voices called out to me.

I whirled around to see Ashley and Abby running toward me. My heart melted to see that—thanks to the witches—the spark had returned in Abby's blue eyes, although she was still very much a vampire, as I was.

Abby jumped into my arms and wrapped her legs around me, nuzzling her face against my neck.

"Thank God you're all right," Ashley said. "None of us had any idea where you had gone. Vivienne's been worrying herself senseless."

"Vivienne? Where is she?" Derek asked.

"I'm not sure. I last saw her about four hours ago. She must be around the island somewhere," Ashley replied.

"Sofia," Derek said, "take Ben. I'm going to look for my sister."

"Where's Ben?" Abby said suddenly, as Derek handed the baby to me and walked back toward the woods.

I knelt down to Abby's level and showed her Ben.

"Here, Abby, this is my son. We named him after your brother," I said, stroking her hair with one hand.

"Ohhh… so you and Mr. Derek made a baby?" Abby looked up at me in wonderment.

"Yes, darling." I smiled, kissing her head. "We made two babies actually." I stood up and caught her hand, walking her over to Aiden. "See? This is my other baby, Rose. She's a girl, and this one's a boy."

"Oh my…" Abby's mouth hung open as she stared at the two identical babies as though they were aliens from another planet. Then, after a few moments' thought, she seemed to reconsider.

"That's gross, Sofia. Because this means that you and Mr. Derek…"

Her voice trailed off and I was thankfully spared whatever embarrassment she was about to subject me to in front of my father. She had taken a look at Aiden. She let out a high-pitched scream.

"Oh! What happened to your dad, Sofia?"

Aiden chuckled as he met Abby's eyes. "I could ask the same of you, little vampire."

"You look like a bird!"

Aiden nodded and stretched out his wings for her.

"Whoa." Abby took a few steps back. "That's so cool. How come you got to be a bird and I didn't?"

"I think being a vampire is better," Aiden said. "You don't get stuck with an ugly beak face."

Abby giggled at that and nodded. "Yeah, I wouldn't want to be a Beak Face."

I took her hand before she could ask more questions and walked her back toward Ashley. Ashley was smiling, but I knew that seeing me with children was a bittersweet experience. She must have been thinking of the family she could have one day had with Sam.

"Hey!" Zinnia's voice sounded out from across the open space. She jogged toward us, Gavin by her side.

"Sweet Jesus, what happened?" Gavin said on seeing the two babies and Aiden as a Hawk.

I recounted the details of our adventure to them as they listened in awe. After I'd finished, Zinnia went up to Aiden and gave him a hug.

"I'm glad you're back, sir." She grinned. "I missed you."

"I guess I missed you too, kiddo." He smiled.

"Um… Sofia?" Gavin's voice now took on a serious tone. "I hope you don't mind, but we held a funeral ceremony while you were gone. All the bereaved families, we needed to do something for them to help soothe their pain. And we didn't want to wait around, what with all the bodies…"

It cut me to the core that I hadn't been there for it. I thought of all the innocent lives lost at the hands of the Elders, people Derek and I were duty-bound to give protection to. I thought of the immunes those evil spirits had managed to sneak through to Cruor already, lives we could never reclaim.

I thought of Sam.

And I thought of Xavier.

I knelt down on the ground and said a prayer, holding a small ceremony of my own for them.

Chapter 40: Vivienne

A gust of sea wind blew against my face, drying the tears and making my eyes sting.

I sat on a high mountain plateau overlooking the most magnificent view of the island. The waves crashing against the shore and the gentle swaying of the redwoods seemed to dance to some kind of untold rhythm.

Peace.

That was what this was. A peace was settling over the ravaged island, slowly drawing its inhabitants back to comfort. Inviting them back to the routine of daily life.

I had a choice whether to let it draw me in too, or whether to continue stirring up the storm within me and cling on to dreams of an impossible future.

I shifted on the ground, moving closer to where I remembered last sitting with Xavier the night he was possessed. I touched the grass next to me, hoping to feel the shape of Xavier's body molded there.

Then I stood up and walked over to the edge of the cliff. And I wondered if, had I not been such a fool and instead given myself to Xavier years before, he would have been stronger in resisting the Elders. I wondered whether my constant resistance had weakened his spirit and resolve to live.

There are some cliffs that are just too late to jump from, Vivienne.

I sat down and dangled my legs off of the edge of the mountain. Then I lay back and gazed up at the stars.

I replayed in my head those last few words we'd exchanged that fateful night, as I'd already done a hundred times since.

"You said you'd wait until I'm ready."

"And I'd do that, Vivienne. You know I would, but..."

But...

"What were you going to say, Xavier?" I whispered out loud, looking up at the stars, hoping his spirit was somehow watching over me. "But... you just wanted to hear it from me? You just wanted to hear me say those three simple words?"

Tears began to stream more heavily down my face.

"Well, I'll say them now to you, Xavier... my love. I love you. I love you. I love you. I love you. I love you." I felt like a crazy person repeating the words over and over again. I'd started in a whisper but soon worked myself up into a frenzy, bellowing against the harsh wind.

"I LOVE YOU, XAVIER!" I screamed until my voice cracked. I broke down, my body utterly exhausted and racked with sobs.

"I love you too."

The smooth baritone voice I ached to hear.

I smiled, my eyes still closed. *Is this what happens when you cherish a memory of someone so much—you start to hear their voice in your head? Then I will cherish you forever, my love, to continue hearing that sweet voice of yours…*

"I love you, Vivienne."

There it was again.

I rolled onto my back and opened my eyes, expecting to take in the beauty of the stars. And while I beheld their beauty, my eyes were met with so much more.

The face of my beloved, staring down at me, a smile etched on his lips. The unshaven face of that beautiful dark-haired man I craved with every fiber of my being.

I reached up, expecting my hand to pass right through the apparition.

"Ouch, Vivienne. That was my eye."

Now you've done it, Vivienne. You've gone mad. You've truly gone mad.

I sat up and looked at the ghost of Xavier. I extended my hand once again, this time aiming for his cheek. It was rough with stubble. I brushed my fingers over his lips. They were soft and moist. I wondered what would happen if I kissed them. Whether I would be able to feel his lips against mine, or whether he might vanish before I could experience such a pleasure.

I didn't need to wait long to find out. Strong arms enveloped my waist and pulled me against him. And then came his kiss. Gentle at first, his lips brushing against the corners of mine, tracing the outline of my mouth, and then increasing in intensity until I was absorbed in his taste.

As I breathed in his scent, tears fell afresh from my eyes. Delirious tears of ecstasy.

"I love you, Xavier… I-I wanted to t-tell you…"

"I know. I know," he whispered into my ear, cupping my face with his large hands. "And, um, I'd be surprised if there's a single person on this island who *doesn't* know after that…"

"Just kiss me."

Chapter 41: Derek

My search for my sister had led me to the side of the island where the submarines were moored. I suspected that perhaps she had retreated into one of them for some peace and quiet. So when I uncovered Xavier's unconscious form lying beneath a bench in one of the old, dilapidated vessels, I almost jumped out of my skin.

At first I believed him to be dead. His body was more wrecked than Sofia's had been when we rescued her, his skin covered with yellow patches, so dry that pieces of it had already flaked off onto the floor.

But when I bent down and placed my ear to his chest, and could just about make out a heartbeat, I was lent at least a small scrap of hope.

I heaved him over my shoulder and sprinted back toward the Port with as much speed as my legs could muster.

"Ibrahim! Ibrahim!" I yelled as I ran through the woods.

Eventually I passed the spot where they were working on the

renovations and the warlock came hurrying toward me.

I laid Xavier's body down on the dirt path and Ibrahim bent over him.

"Corrine!" he shouted. "I'm going to need your help with this one."

"Good grief," Corrine murmured, taking in Xavier's appearance.

"Please!" I gasped, falling to my knees. "Just tell me you can save him. Just say the words, I beg of you!"

But neither of them said anything to me. I closed my eyes. It was too painful to watch them struggle to save him. I just wanted to open my eyes again once they'd fixed him.

I heard Corrine calling more witches over to assist them. More than twenty minutes must have passed, with half a dozen witches muttering chants at the same time. The hope I had for his survival was slipping away from me by the second.

But then I reminded myself, *I know my friend. And I know that he's a survivor.* So half an hour later, when he came to and sat up, part of me wasn't surprised.

He looked around with a bewildered expression on his face. I rushed to him and grabbed his shoulders, pulling him into a tight embrace.

"Thank heavens," I whispered. "How the hell did you end up in that submarine?"

"I-I..." He rubbed his eyes as if trying to clear his mind. "I crawled. My Elder left me for Sofia... it left me lying inside the temple. Somehow, I managed to crawl there undetected."

As soon as he had regained enough balance to stand on his own two feet, he asked anxiously, "Where's Vivienne?"

"She's alive and on the island. I was just looking for her, in fact."

And then he sped off into the darkness of the woods without

another word. Trusting that Xavier would find Vivienne soon enough, I was eager to return to Sofia, to my new family.

She was where I had left her, in the clearing outside the Cells. She sat in a circle with Aiden, Ashley and Abby. Kyle, Ian and Anna also sat nearby along with two other couples; Cameron and Liana, and Gavin and Zinnia.

I'd noted Yuri and Claudia's absence ever since we'd arrived back on the island. Though I didn't need to put much thought into where they might be. Although our new Residences weren't ready yet, I knew that any enclosed area would be more than suitable for their needs.

On seeing me approach, Abby shrieked with laughter. "Hello, Mr. Derek! I know what you and Sofia did…"

"Tell me, Miss Abby. What did we do?" Although I spoke to Abby, I looked at Sofia, a suggestive smile forming on my lips.

"You gave each other babies!" She pointed to the twins who were both resting in Aiden's arms.

Sofia giggled and her face flushed, not quite as bright as it would have if she were still a human, but exceptionally bright for a vampire.

"Huh, really? Is that what happened now?" I sat down next to Sofia and pulled her between my legs, snaking my arms around her waist and holding her tight against my chest. "And is there anything wrong with that, Miss Abby?"

Sofia gripped my knee, begging me to stop encouraging Abby in front of everyone.

"Well, that depends how you did it, Mister. Did you pray to angels or"—Abby winked—"did you kiss her belly button?"

Everyone in the group roared with laughter.

"Oh dear, I kissed her belly button. Am I in trouble with you, Miss Abby?"

"Yes!" she squealed, wagging a finger at me. "Because that's the gross one!"

"Oh dear, dear, dear," I muttered, just loud enough for Sofia to hear. "Because I might just want to kiss her belly button again."

Sofia shushed me, still giggling. I pressed my lips against the back of her cold neck and stood up, lifting her up with me. I held her hand and said to the others, "We'll see you in a bit."

Then I walked her over to a quiet spot in the woods, away from the construction sounds of wood clanking and glass chinking. I led her to a tree and pressed her against it. I caught her lips with mine and kissed her, tasting her coldness in my mouth.

"And now?" I looked down into her eyes, a serious expression falling over my face. "How will I ever kiss your lovely belly button again?"

She giggled, then touched my cheek and said, "More like, how am I going to breastfeed our babies while I'm a vampire? I don't want them to grow up without ever having their mother's milk. And how will I build sandcastles with them?"

"And what will happen when I'm an old man? You'll want to swap me for a younger model," I teased.

"But seriously, Derek." She stopped laughing. "What are we going to do? I can't remain a vampire."

I stepped back from her a little and sighed. "I don't know. My greatest fear is losing you again."

"Well, the cure worked on both you and Kyle. Why shouldn't it work on me? We've no evidence that I'm any different a vampire than you or Kyle were. Yes, I was turned in Cruor, and yes, I was an immune... but the whole point is that my immunity was broken down and I became normal. That's how I was turned in the first place. And it's the same disease. Plus, we have our immune, Anna.

She won't mind giving me some of her blood."

The thought of Sofia undergoing the same torture I had made me ache inside. "The pain is excruciating. Unlike anything you can imagine. I don't... I just don't know if I can handle putting you through that," I said.

"Well, Mr. Derek, you're just going to have to toughen up if you ever want to kiss my belly button again." She lifted my chin up so that I was facing her. She kissed my cheek and said, "Look, I've already been to hell and back. Believe me when I say that one more burn isn't going to make a lot of difference."

I grinned but couldn't deny that her words hurt at the same time. "I guess not," I said. "I haven't exactly done a good job at keeping you safe from harm."

"Oh, don't go into this whole self-blame thing again. I knew what I was getting myself into when I married you." She pulled my head down toward her and kissed me again. "Now, if it's all right with you, I'd like to get this over with."

Chapter 42: Derek

Aiden protested at first, but Sofia persuaded him. We left the twins with him and walked with Anna toward the Pit, the one tiny area of the island where the sun shone through. Others wanted to accompany us, but Sofia refused them all. She wanted only Anna and myself.

She barely said a word as we walked. A determined expression set on her face as we marched her up to the entrance of the Pit. She didn't want to make a "big fuss" out of it as we had done with my own turning.

Even when I went to hug her, she pulled away, as though she didn't want to even consider that she might not see me again.

Anna bared her neck to her, and Sofia dug her fangs in and took a sip. She licked her lips and waited a few minutes for the blood to enter her system. Then she stepped through the doors to the Pit and slammed them behind her.

And then the screaming began. I now understood what it must

have been like for Sofia to witness me undergoing such a procedure. Hours and hours passed by. Even though her voice had grown hoarse, she still cried out.

Anna stayed with me the whole time, laying a hand on my shoulder. I tried to draw comfort from her, but it was impossible. Eventually the only way I could cope was by curling up into a ball on the ground and cupping my hands over my ears.

Finally, Sofia's noises stopped. I was tempted to barge in to check what was happening, but then the doors creaked open themselves.

Sofia, in all her mortal glory, emerged from the bright pit, stumbling into my arms. She looked exhausted, but at the same time, to my great relief, she had a vibrant glow.

"So," she gasped. "About going to hell and back? Huh. Yeah, now I can say I've *officially* done that."

Chapter 43: Sofia

I slept for ten hours after my turning; my body had been crying out for sleep. Derek took me to an empty room in the Catacombs that was still in decent condition. He sat by my bed as I fell asleep, and was still there when I awoke.

Aiden also sat beside me, still cradling his beloved grandchildren. And then my eyes fell on Xavier and Vivienne. They sat in a corner wrapped in each other's arms.

"Xavier!" I cried out. I jumped up and ran over to him, pulling him into a hug.

I could say with absolute certainty that I had never seen Vivienne so happy. She beamed as she looked at me. I clasped her to me and kissed her cheek again and again, until she'd finally had enough of my affection and said, "Hey, girl, it's Xavier I'm marrying, not you. And besides, look at Derek. You're making him all jealous."

"Oh, I can't wait for your wedding! Can we have it tomorrow?" I squealed, sounding not dissimilar to Abby.

"Yes, actually," Xavier answered with a grin. "This girl just can't get enough of me. She would marry me right now if she could. I mean, she didn't even give me a chance to get down on one knee and propose properly!"

Vivienne affectionately brushed a strand of hair away from his face.

I started thinking over all the preparations that would need to be made, and realized that we might just be able to pull it off now Corrine had her powers back.

And so the countdown began.

"Okay, men. Leave this room. Now!" I turned to Derek who was eyeing me with amusement. "Oh wait, actually, Derek, do you know if the witches have finished with any of the renovations yet?"

"You'll be glad to know that all the tree houses are done. Corrine tells me they're magnificent, although I haven't seen them myself yet. And they're now working on the humans' housing."

"Well then, we can leave this crummy room and have a proper space for my bride to get ready in. Derek, take Xavier and at least try to make him.... *somewhat* presentable for my ravishing bride."

"You say that with such low confidence." Derek mocked being offended. "Just you wait and see, loudmouth. I'll make him into a more beautiful groom than she will be a bride."

With that, he grabbed Xavier—who now looked mildly alarmed at Derek's threat of "beautification" —and marched him out of the room. They were headed to Derek's penthouse, I assumed.

I kissed both of my babies, who were still asleep, then pecked my father on the cheek. I asked him to follow us to Vivienne's penthouse since I wanted my twins close to me. I grabbed Vivienne's hand and we all walked out of the room.

"Come on, hurry," I said. "We can't give Derek any head start.

Who knows what he's got up his sleeve."

As soon as we were out in the open, Aiden spread his wings and launched into the sky. Vivienne let out a rich laugh and sped up. I had forgotten that I now had human legs and she soon tired of me lagging behind. She pulled me onto her back and we dashed through the woods. We saw Xavier and Derek ahead of us, rushing toward the same direction.

When Vivienne took a giant leap upward and we landed on her verandah in the Residences, I looked around in awe. The penthouses seemed larger and more beautiful than I had ever remembered them. Pots of exotic flowers lined the balconies and entryways. Fountains gushed in the center of the verandahs.

Aiden touched down soon afterward. He took the twins into a quiet spare bedroom where they could sleep peacefully, and stayed there watching over them.

I escorted Vivienne into her stunning new bedroom, but then remembered in annoyance that I needed Corrine.

"Relax and have a bath or something, okay? We need Corrine."

Vivienne smiled at me and nodded.

I walked back out onto the verandah and shouted across to Derek's penthouse on the other side of a stretch of trees.

"Hey, Mr. Derek!" I shouted. His head peeked out of a window. "Run and get Corrine for me, will you?"

"Get her yourself!" he called back. "I'm not helping you get any advantage over Xavier and me. Vivienne's too pretty even without any makeup. And don't disturb us again. Can't you see we're extremely busy?" He and Xavier both howled with laughter as he slammed the window shut.

I chuckled and muttered, "Boys," beneath my breath.

In the end I had to disturb Vivienne to run and fetch Corrine, considering it might have taken me hours to search her out as a human and Aiden was inseparable from the twins.

Once Corrine had arrived, we started making progress. We took Vivienne's measurements, and within half an hour, Corrine had conjured up the most beautiful wedding dress I'd ever laid eyes on. It rivaled even my own. Then we had a makeup and hair rehearsal session, and once we were sure we'd got it just right, Corrine and I left Vivienne alone to have some peace before the real event.

As Corrine and I took the elevator down to the ground and walked away from Vivienne's penthouse to decide where to actually host the wedding, Derek came running toward us.

"And what do *you* want?" I asked, cocking my head to the side.

"Firstly, I want *you*, Mrs. Belly-Button." He knocked the breath right out of me as he picked me up, swinging me around in the air before finally landing a kiss on my lips. He put me back on the ground before continuing. "Secondly, I know where we should host the wedding. Up on the mountaintop where Xavier found Vivienne. Come on, I'll show you."

"What about your blushing groom?" Corrine smirked. "You sure he can manage his blow-dry without you?"

We giggled and made our way to the plateau where Corrine started conjuring up seats and tents and thousands of white roses. Derek offered the occasional suggestion, but he was wise enough to leave the majority of decisions to us.

Once we'd sorted out the venue, Corrine and I returned to Vivienne and Derek to Xavier. The three of us barely slept that night. In between running back and forth to the spare bedroom to check on my babies, the final preparations went by quickly. Before we knew it, we had Vivienne standing in front of the mirror, dressed and looking breathtaking.

We made sure that Xavier and Derek made their way up to the mountain first, before they could set eyes on Vivienne.

Once we arrived at the end of the aisle, a warm sea breeze catching Vivienne's veil, hundreds of seats were filled with vampires and humans alike. I spotted dozens of familiar faces in the crowds, but sitting in the seats closest to the aisle and the altar were Claudia and Yuri; Cameron and Liana; Kyle and Anna; Gavin and Zinnia; Abby sitting on Ashley's lap with Landis next to them; and my father right at the front with my two little cherubs.

Although Derek attempted to swing a pink flower garland over Xavier's head just as Vivienne was about to start walking down the aisle, I was relieved to see that he hadn't done anything outrageous to the groom's appearance. I suspected actually that Derek had nothing to do with Xavier's smart black tuxedo and gelled-back hair, and that rather Ibrahim was behind it all.

I caught Derek's eye, and mouthed, *I won.*

He took one look at Vivienne and nodded back.

Vivienne reached Xavier, and Ibrahim conducted the ceremony. They exchanged rings and when it finally came time to kiss, the crowds erupted with cheers. Then to everyone's surprise, Vivienne yelled out at the top of her lungs, "I love you, Xavier!"

She threw her bouquet into the crowd. Abby dove for it with her vampire speed and a huge goofy smile spread across her face when she caught it.

Tears glinted in both of the newlyweds' eyes as they enveloped themselves in each other's arms and kissed once again.

As if the crowds weren't already going wild enough, Ibrahim caught hold of Corrine, whisked her up in his arms and stood her at the side of the altar. Then he bent down on one knee, reached into his pocket and withdrew a large diamond ring. Corrine's face became the color of a raspberry and she looked as though she was about to hyperventilate.

"Oh, God," she gasped. "Ibrahim, oh, you…" For once, Corrine had been rendered speechless by a male. "Yes!" she shouted finally. Ibrahim put the heavy engagement ring on her finger and drew her against his body, kissing her in front of everyone and not attempting to hide the heat of his embrace one little bit. Corrine responded with abandon.

Wolf-whistles abounded, the cheers and clapping deafening.

"Gate-crashers!" Zinnia yelled through the crowds, laughing and pumping her fist in the air.

"Well, if they're doing it…" Gavin grabbed Zinnia's arm and tugged on her to stand up. I gasped and thought for a moment that he was about to propose, but instead he said, "Come on! Let's make out!"

Zinnia howled with laughter, but followed him up onto the altar next to the two already kissing couples, and they began eating each other's faces off.

It didn't take much more encouragement for Claudia to haul Yuri up to the stage; now there were four kissing couples.

Oh, no…

I had been avoiding looking toward Derek's direction, but he was having none of it. He made his way over to me and grabbed me by the waist. He carried me up to the altar and stood us next to Xavier and Vivienne.

"Oh, what the heck!" I said, brushing away all embarrassment I had about letting myself go in front of Aiden, and eased myself into Derek's embrace.

I was half expecting more couples to join us, but with ten people already on stage, and Yuri and Claudia being particularly carefree in their motions, there really wasn't any more room.

Instead, couples began standing up in their seats or wherever else there was space. In between Derek's affections, I was thrilled to see Cameron and Liana sharing a kiss in the aisle. And then Kyle and Anna.

On spotting Ashley still seated, trying to smile but clearly failing at it, I shouted out. "Okay, enough! Let's have some music!"

A group of witches took up some instruments and began playing a beautiful slow melody. I was relieved to see Landis be a gentleman and lead Ashley to a dance.

Abby, feeling left out, made her way over to Aiden and the twins to ask them to dance. Derek and I laughed as my father did the best he could to satisfy her with two babies in his arms.

I danced with Derek for over an hour, but eventually pulled him away from the dance floor. We walked over to Aiden. The ever-enthusiastic Abby had now given him a break and preoccupied herself with a game of chase with Shadow, upending tables and leaving a trail of chaos behind them as they ran. I giggled as Eli chased after the dog, trying to reattach his leash.

I took Ben from my father, while Derek took Rose. We walked to find a quieter spot away from the crowds and dancing, but which still allowed us a good view over the festivities.

Derek didn't ask what I was doing. One look in his eyes, and I could tell he had already sensed what I was dying for. I sat between Derek's legs and leaned my back against his chest, placing both twins on my lap. I loosened the straps of my dress and asked him to hold up a tablecloth to cover me.

And then I fed our two little babies. I finally allowed myself the simple pleasure my body had been crying out for ever since I'd been separated from them all that time ago.

Derek kissed my shoulders and rocked us gently from side to side, humming a haunting melody into my ear beneath the loud party music.

Our melody.

Chapter 44: Sofia

Derek and I sat on the beach outside our Californian dream home. I held Rose in my arms while Derek held Ben. We'd fixed an umbrella over our heads to protect the babies from the midday sun and positioned them upright so they could look out at the sparkling ocean. Watching the other children playing in the waves, I felt excited for the day Ben and Rose would be old enough to join them and build sandcastles with us.

I took a bite from one of the peaches we'd packed in the hamper and looked over at Derek. Despite their color, his eyes were filled with warmth.

"We did it," I said softly, clutching his hand in mine. "Is this how you imagined it would be? *True sanctuary?*"

Derek reached for my face and caressed my cheek with his thumb. He placed a tender kiss on my lips.

"It's everything I imagined... and so much more," he whispered.

After Vivienne and Xavier's wedding, things settled into more of a routine in The Shade. The humans' residences were finished and I almost cried with joy upon seeing what a thoughtful job the witches had done. They'd created town houses, much like you'd see in any city, with all the amenities that a human could need.

Playgrounds were created for children. A group of witches even started up a school for them, which Abby eagerly attended.

Ibrahim and Corrine managed to figure out a way to modify Cora's spell to allow the sun to stream down onto a small stretch of beach, north of the island. Humans lounging around there, swimming in the sea and getting a tan, soon became a common sight.

But more than any of this, we instituted a law that any human was allowed to leave The Shade at any time. I persuaded Derek that even if they went to the police, there was no way they could ever find us. And, in any case, I trusted that most of the humans would not wish us harm any more. For The Shade was no longer the cruel dictatorship it once was. They were no longer treated as slaves, but as citizens.

A good number of the humans jumped at the opportunity and left, but a surprising number stayed.

Vampires remained vampires for the time being. They'd always have the opportunity to turn at a later time. And I certainly wasn't ready to subject Abby to such pain. I drew comfort knowing that turning was always a possibility in the future should she insist upon it.

As for my father, he set out on a mission with Zinnia and Gavin to disperse the hunters seeing that there was now nothing left to hunt for. The Elders had gone and the Hawks, for whom they had been unknowing puppets, were exiled too. The hunters' already shaky mission statement had just lost its last legs.

We still hadn't figured out if there was a way to turn Aiden back into a human. Ibrahim could give him the *appearance* of a human temporarily, but even he didn't know how to truly turn my father back. However, as Aiden himself pointed out, there was no hurry to find a cure for him, other than to save him from the terrible shame and embarrassment of having Abby permanently nickname him "Beak Face".

Derek and I, along with the twins, split our time between our Californian dream home, where Derek indulged in his newfound hobby of cooking, and ruling The Shade. Xavier and Vivienne managed the island whenever we took breaks away from it.

Although our life seemed like it couldn't be more perfect, I never grew complacent. I never forgot for a moment all that we had suffered and sacrificed to achieve what we had.

I also knew that nothing in this life was certain. When Shadow discovered a strange creature washed up on the shores of The Shade, during a morning walk with Eli, it confirmed that belief for me. Eli declared it to be the body of a werewolf.

Ibrahim confirmed that it was possible the Ancients had accidentally opened more portals between Earth and other unknown realms than even they themselves had realized. But he also offered us assurance that most supernatural creatures were not domineering and aggressive like the Hawks and Elders. He said that many were harmless to humans.

Harmless or not, whatever the case, I know that I can't control the future.

I can't control the world. I can't make the world a safe place for my children. Derek and I still don't know what powers they might grow up to possess, and what the consequences of such abilities might be.

They may face trouble and they may struggle. They may even encounter darkness and evil. I cannot change that. That is beyond my control.

What I can do, however, is show them that where there is darkness, there is light. Where there is evil, there is good.

They may face disturbance and conflict, yes... but they can also encounter beauty and bliss. I can assure them that no matter what happens, they can always hope that there's something worth living for in this world.

All of the bad and good things that come with living become worthwhile once we find love. I should know.

I found it in the most unlikely of places, didn't I?

Epilogue: Kiev

Why did I let her go?

It was a question that had been plaguing my mind ever since I'd placed that kiss on her forehead.

I just let her... slip through my fingers. Why?

I lay on the damp floor and looked up at the wooden ceiling. The heat and humidity of the cell I'd been locked in weighed down on my chest.

I reached for my back and traced my fingers across the deep wounds Arron had inflicted on me for allowing them to escape.

Then I let my eyelids fall shut. Emerald-green irises flashed before me in my mind's eye.

You don't care about her. Just like you never cared about Natalie.

And yet I wanted her still. Even though I knew from the way she'd looked at me that I disgusted her.

Part of me had wanted her to save me from myself.

But then I'd caught the vision of my own red eyes reflected in her teary pupils.

And I'd known that she couldn't save me.

I would only end up dragging her down with me, just as I had done with Natalie. And the countless other women who'd crossed paths with me.

As I lay in the darkness, I wondered if there truly was anyone, in any realm, whom I could love without ruining.

"The night is darkest before dawn breaks."

Dear Shaddict,

I'm writing this note to you after I've literally just typed the last word.

This book is likely to be the conclusion of Derek and Sofia's story arc. I say this with tears in my eyes, because yes, I will miss them both dearly.

That said, I don't plan to abandon the world of The Shade.

There are other characters who simply won't leave me in peace until I've told their stories.

Kiev is one such character.

When I first wrote Kiev into the series, I honestly didn't expect much from him. But as the series progressed, his character began haunting me more and more.

Why did he take Ben? How and why did he go to Aviary, and what will happen to him next?

How did he become the man he is today?

Is he even capable of a Happy Ever After?

There's a side to Kiev that I find even more interesting and intriguing than our beloved Derek.

I look forward to exploring these questions myself and sharing his story with you in my next book... A Shade of Kiev!

Please visit www.bellaforrest.net for information on how to purchase it.

All my love,

Bella (and everyone else in the world of The Shade, both living and deceased).

P.S. You may meet Sofia and Derek again in future books and learn more about the twins.

P.P.S. If you sign up to my "new releases" email list, you'll automatically stay updated about all my future releases: www.forrestbooks.com

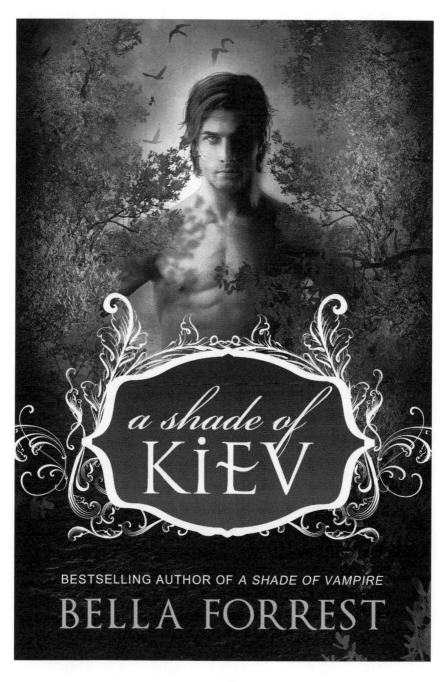

Visit **www.bellaforrest.net** for more information.

Made in the USA
San Bernardino, CA
30 July 2014